Reclaiming Tomorrow

by

Jade Winters

Reclaiming Tomorrow

By Jade Winters

Published by Wicked Winters Books

Copyright © 2023 Jade Winters

www.jade-winters.com

All rights reserved. This book or any portion thereof may not be reproduced or used in any manner whatsoever without the express written permission of the author.

All characters in this publication are fictitious and any resemblance to real persons, living or dead, is purely coincidental.

ISBN: 979-8-861-86302-5

Other titles by Jade Winters

Novels

Under Her Gaze
No Other Love
Falling
All That Matters
Missing Pieces
143
Caught by Love
Guilty Hearts
Say Something
Faking it
Second Thoughts
Just One Destiny
Unravelled
Picking the Right Heart
The Second Time
Secrets
In it Together
Love Interrupted
The Song, The Heart
Accidentally Together
Flirting with Danger
Unravelled
Lost in You
Starting Over Again
You and Me
Just One Mistake

Novellas

Talk Me Down from the Edge
From That Day

The Ashley McCoy Detective Series

Sixty Seconds
A Walk into Darkness
Everything to Lose

Amber Hills Series

Love's Knocking
Always You

Looking for Ms Right Series

Looking for Ms Right
Torn
The Chase

Chapter One

Parishioners sought refuge from the downpour beneath the church's eaves while blackbirds flocked above, squawking in an eerie symphony that mirrored the sombre atmosphere below. The congregation stood close together, tightly gripping their umbrellas. Moments later, the loud metallic clang of the church door unlocking jolted the solemn silence. The heavy door swung wide, revealing an elderly woman with weathered lines etched upon her face, each wrinkle telling the story of a well-lived life. She beckoned the congregants inside, and they filed past her slowly, finding their way to their respective pews guided by a quiet sense of reverence.

Josh and Lindsay Miller arrived at the church just as the service began. Lindsay typically prided herself on her punctuality, so today's tardiness was a break from the norm. Their baby daughter, Chloe, had come down with a fever, and her symptoms had worsened during the night, keeping the entire household awake. Neither Josh, Lindsay, nor their eighteen-year-old daughter, Sasha, had heard the alarm clock in their exhausted state.

Once the initial blame game subsided, the urgency to make it to church on time outweighed the need to find a suitable scapegoat for their predicament. Lindsay hastily dressed in her pencil skirt and tapered blazer, adorning her neck with her favourite twenty-two-carat gold cross. Although she had intended to wash her hair before church, their lateness left her no choice but to hastily pin her blond locks into a bun and apply an extra touch of rouge to conceal her sleep-deprived pallor.

Hurriedly entering the church just as the priest ascended the pulpit, Josh and Lindsay offered apologetic nods to those who turned their heads and smiled at the sight of the Millers sneaking in. After the hour-long service, they made their way to the rectory, where much-needed coffee was being served.

'I see time got the better of you today, Josh?' Reverend Howard jested, giving a friendly pat on Josh Miller's back.

'Yeah, Lindsay …' Josh began, but his words trailed off as he caught Lindsay's gaze. 'I mean, I forgot to set the alarm. Chloe had a rough night.'

'Poor little thing. Is she still unwell?' the priest asked, his eyes filled with sympathy.

'Unfortunately,' Josh replied. 'We'll keep an eye on her tonight before deciding if we should take her to the doctor. If Lindsay and I lose any more sleep, we'll be known as the "Dream Team", because we'll be dreaming of getting some actual sleep!'

As Josh and Reverend Howard exchanged light-hearted banter about the effects of sleep deprivation, Lindsay poured herself another cup of coffee and settled on the edge of a sofa near the window. The rays of sunlight filtered through the glass, offering a soothing warmth upon her face. Before long, her weary eyes closed for a brief moment.

'Oh my god!' a woman exclaimed beside her, jolting Lindsay from her momentary stupor. The woman quickly corrected herself, noticing the curious gazes directed her way. 'Um … goodness, I mean.'

Fully alert now, Lindsay stared at the startled woman with dishevelled hair and a pretty yellow blouse now stained with coffee. Lindsay had inadvertently spilled the contents of her cup on the unsuspecting woman during her momentary lapse.

'I'm so, so sorry!' Lindsay apologised profusely.

Without hesitation, Lindsay reached into her bag and retrieved a tissue.

'I'll pay for the dry cleaning,' Lindsay offered as she delicately pressed the tissue against the fabric, gently blotting the coffee stain in an attempt to salvage what she could of the blouse's original colour.

The woman's initial surprise dissolved into a smile of reassurance.

'No, it's fine. It's an old blouse anyway.' She sighed, her tone carrying a touch of resignation. She ran a hand through her hair, the strands falling back into place as if surrendering to their natural chaos.

'I can be a right scatterbrain when I'm sleep-deprived,' Lindsay confessed, her smile filled with self-deprecation. 'Baby has kept us up all night.'

'Oh, you must feel awful,' the woman said.

'I do. I used to dream of a big family, but these last few days have made me think I might just stick with two.'

The woman's eyes met Lindsay's, filled with

empathy. 'I get that. Life tends to mess with our plans, and sometimes we have to adjust our perspective and embrace the hand we're dealt.'

Lost in their brief but profound connection, Lindsay realised she hadn't properly introduced herself.

'I'm Lindsay, by the way,' she said, extending her hand towards the woman.

Accepting the gesture, the woman offered a warm smile. 'Christine.'

'You're new here, aren't you? I haven't seen you around before.'

'I recently moved to the area. Then, I went to a residential camp, and I only got back a few days ago. So, you're catching me on my first-ever church visit,' Christine explained, a hint of tiredness creeping into her words.

'Residential camp?' Lindsay questioned, raising an eyebrow in curiosity as she took a sip of her coffee, the warmth spreading comfortably through her body.

'Yeah, we provide guidance and support for kids under eighteen who might be going through some tough times in their lives.'

'Oh, right. Are you a counsellor?' Lindsay enquired, her interest piqued.

There was a brief pause as Christine's eyes wandered to a point in the distance, outside the window.

'I'm actually a volunteer mentor in my spare time,' she finally said, her voice softening with introspection. 'During these camps, we usually team up with different organisations to tackle the challenges young people face.'

'That sounds like a great initiative,' Lindsay said.

Christine let out a sigh, her voice carrying a touch of frustration.

'Sometimes I just feel so powerless, you know? There are these kids who seem to be really struggling. They're dealing with emotional ups and downs, and they're just not getting the guidance they need. But, honestly, it's not really their fault. It's on society to step in and help them recover from the effects of bad parenting.'

'Absolutely,' Lindsay agreed wholeheartedly. 'It must be really hard to watch them go through all that and feel like there's not much they can do about it.'

Christine's eyes held a glimmer of vulnerability as she met Lindsay's gaze.

'It really is, more than I'd like to admit. Like, I've been mentoring this incredible young woman who's on the brink of leaving her foster home,' Christine revealed, worry evident in her tone. 'I really wish I could help her transition into the real world on her own, but honestly, I travel a lot with work, and just don't have enough free time to help her as much as I'd like.'

'What kind of help does she need?'

'Things like managing finances, finding stable housing, and even navigating job opportunities. She's got the drive, but without proper guidance, it's a daunting task. She said she doesn't feel ready to live on her own just yet, but she doesn't want to live in a hostel either.'

'Christine, how old is she?' Lindsay enquired, a

spark of an idea taking shape in her mind. She stole a glance at Josh, who was deeply engaged in conversation with the reverend. She knew he wouldn't be thrilled, but she also knew he'd relent eventually, as he always did.

Christine's brows knitted together. 'Just turned eighteen a few weeks back. Why do you ask?'

'Well, I was thinking … if she needs a positive role model to set her on the right path …' Her voice trailed off momentarily. '… we would be more than willing to take her in. I mean, if you think it would be beneficial for her.'

Christine locked eyes with Lindsay. 'Are you serious? You'd do that?'

'Yep, I think I'd be up for it. My eldest daughter is the same age, so maybe this could be a good thing for both of them,' Lindsay explained, reaching into her purse and producing a business card with her contact details. She handed it to Christine. 'Take a moment to talk to her, and if she's interested, give me a call. We can figure out the details together.'

Christine's eyes drifted down to the card, her voice tinged with a touch of disbelief. 'Wait, hold on. You're an author of parenting books?'

'Yeah, I figured I could make a difference by helping people in whatever way I can. Turns out, supporting struggling parents through my books is one way to do that.'

'Wow, I'm seriously impressed,' Christine said, a genuine sense of admiration in her voice.

Lindsay modestly waved off the compliment.

'Oh, come on, what I do is really nothing compared to your work. Seriously, there's no contest. That's why I'm totally on board to help if I can. We both have the chance to make a real difference in someone's life, and if I can do my part, it's like I'm fulfilling my purpose. We've got the room, and let's be honest, an eighteen-year-old doesn't need constant supervision – just some emotional support.'

'That's precisely it! Just someone to show they care, Lindsay. If we can make this happen, it would mean everything to both of us,' Christine said, her voice catching with emotion.

Lindsay extended her hand, placing it comfortingly on Christine's shoulder. 'I truly believe that everyone deserves an opportunity for a better life. And if we have the chance to offer that to her, then we should seize it.'

'In that case, I'll reach out soon.'

As Lindsay stood up, she looked down at Christine, a warm smile on her lips.

'The sooner, the better.'

Chapter Two

Hailey sat alone at a corner table in the busy café, nervously tapping her fingers on the smooth surface of the wooden table. The clinking of cutlery and the low murmur of conversations surrounded her as she stole glances at the bustling street outside. It had been only a few weeks since she turned eighteen, and she would soon be leaving the foster care system behind. Though this brought a sense of freedom, the weight of uncertainty pressed heavily upon her shoulders.

Christine, her mentor, had called her a few days ago with an air of excitement in her voice. She promised Hailey a surprise, a glimmer of hope in a world that had often seemed dim. But as the minutes ticked by, Hailey's apprehension grew. What could Christine possibly have in store for her?

Lost in contemplation, Hailey absentmindedly twisted a strand of her hair around her finger. Her mind wandered through thoughts of the future, navigating life's intricacies and the roads yet untravelled. Her past troubles had left an indelible mark, instilling a cautious uncertainty about what lay ahead. Was this surprise a genuine chance at the new beginning she yearned for, or would it dissolve into yet another fleeting mirage of happiness?

The door swung open, capturing Hailey's attention in an instant. In walked Christine, a vibrant aura emanating from her every step. Her unruly auburn curls framed her face like a halo of fire.

'Hailey!' Christine said as she strode purposefully across the room. 'Do I have some fantastic news for you or what!'

'I can't wait to hear it,' Hailey said, smiling up at her.

After a brief hug, Christine slid into the chair opposite Hailey. 'I've found you a place to live – a fresh start with a family who want to help you get on your feet.'

'Really?' Scepticism lingered in Hailey's voice as she looked at Christine.

'Yes, really.'

'Okay … I mean … wow, that's great news. Who are they?'

'They're a wonderful couple I met at church,' Christine said. 'They have two daughters, one your age and a six-month-old. The father is a teacher, and the mother – hold onto your seat – is an author.'

'Wow, I've never met an actual author before.' Hailey's voice was tinged with awe. The thought of meeting someone who brought worlds to life through their words seemed almost surreal.

Christine laughed softly, the sound warm and genuine. 'Neither had I until a few days ago.'

'I … I genuinely don't know what to say …'

Hailey's gaze dropped to the swirling patterns on the café floor. She considered the weight of her decision, her inner dialogue spinning with questions and doubts. What if this family was just another fleeting refuge, just another brief pause in her turbulent journey?

As if reading her mind, Christine leaned forward, her voice filled with earnest sincerity. 'I know you've been through so much, Hailey, and trust is hard to come by. But I promise you, this family is different.'

Hailey looked up and met Christine's steadfast gaze, brimming with compassion and unwavering belief. In that moment, Hailey knew she had to take a leap of faith.

'You're willing to give it a go?'

With a tentative smile, Hailey nodded and said, 'Sure. What have I got to lose?'

Chapter Three

The street ahead was lined with majestic oak trees, forming a protective canopy as Sasha walked, exhaustion weighing down her steps. Strands of hair playfully danced in front of her face, and with an exasperated huff, she cleared her view.

Replaying the day's events, Sasha's mind wandered. University had drained her, but she had eagerly attended her last class, drawn by the allure of Dr Anderson, her enigmatic personal tutor.

Sasha's cheeks flushed at the thought. Dr Anderson's magnetic charm and piercing gaze ignited a fire within her. With tousled hair and captivating eyes, she exuded an air of mystery that tantalised Sasha's imagination. She yearned to be noticed by her, but how could Sasha, just an ordinary teenager, capture the attention of someone like Dr Anderson? It felt like an impossible dream.

At eighteen, the yearning for simple gestures of affection – a tender kiss, the comforting warmth of love – seemed almost bittersweet. In the midst of these feelings, Dr Anderson, her first crush, appeared like the perfect candidate to satisfy those cravings.

As her house came into view, Sasha's spirits dampened. Dark clouds gathered overhead, and rain began to fall. She quickened her pace, mirroring the urgency of the atmosphere.

Inside, Sasha's anticipation for the chocolate cake she had put aside turned to disappointment – it was nowhere to be found. Scouring the fridge, her frustration grew.

'Isn't anything sacred in this house?' she muttered to herself.

She settled for two hearty sandwiches, generously stuffed with succulent ham, a hint of mustard, and a large gherkin. It was a poor consolation for the missing cake.

Sasha ascended the stairs to her bedroom and sat comfortably on her bed. With a sandwich in hand, she opened a book and was drawn into the fascination of ancient Egypt.

Soon, her father's four-by-four engine hummed in the driveway. The front door slammed, and distant rumblings followed between her parents.

Her father's voice broke the room's tranquillity. 'Hey, Sash! We're home!'

Sasha's fingers tightened around the book as his footsteps climbed the stairs. The door opened, her apprehensive greeting one of resignation. His presence invaded her sanctuary.

'Do you want to come with us to your mum's book reading tonight?' he asked, an unexpected invitation.

Sasha hesitated, her mind racing for an excuse that satisfied them both.

'Um, no thanks, I'm tired,' she replied, masking unease with a smile. 'But I'm happy to look after Chloe while you and Mum go.'

Frustration flickered on her father's features,

hidden behind a leer. 'You can't keep an eye on Chloe forever, you know?'

The words hung heavily.

That's where you're wrong. I can and I will. Though she thought it, she remained silent.

He leaned against the doorframe. Sasha resisted the urge to ask him to leave, knowing the response.

'Are you sure you won't change your mind?' he pressed.

Sasha held her resentment beneath the surface. 'Positive,' she replied.

'Your mum isn't going to like this. Not one little bit.'

Their eyes locked, a silent battle. Her father straightened, stepping back.

'Suit yourself,' he conceded, resignation in his tone. 'We aren't leaving until six.'

As her father's footsteps faded, Sasha closed her eyes, burdened by the world's weight. What would she do? The question echoed, offering no answers.

Chapter Four

Hailey perched on her bed's edge, anticipation and nostalgia weighing on her heart. Her room, a haven for the past year, now felt both familiar and foreign – a snapshot of a chapter about to close. The walls, once adorned with posters and memories, stood bare, boxes stacked, waiting for the inevitable change.

Her fingers traced the desk's grooves, memories of late-night studies etched in the wood. A song's echo hummed in her mind, a faithful companion through highs and lows. This room had offered solace, a retreat from the world's turmoil. Soon it would be time to say goodbye.

A soft knock broke her reverie; Mrs Wilson stood in the doorway.

'Nearly all packed, I see.'

'Yeah, I didn't realise it would be this quick.'

Truth was, she was eager to leave. Another foster kid was lined up to take her place. Transitioning smoothly seemed best for both of them.

Though Mrs Wilson had offered stability, their bond wasn't strong. Hailey had arrived at seventeen, scars from a turbulent past overshadowing progress.

'I know this is tough, Hailey. But it's your chance for a fresh start. You deserve it.' Mrs Wilson's words held warmth.

'Thanks for opening your home to me.'

'I'm glad I could help. I'll get dinner started. Pasta tonight,' Mrs Wilson said, departing, leaving Hailey alone.

As the evening sun cast a warm, golden glow through the window, Hailey's gaze settled on a faded photograph resting on the dressing table. It captured a moment of laughter shared with Maggie, her first adoptive mother, their smiles frozen in time. A bittersweet smile tugged at her lips, and she picked up the photograph, her fingers trembling slightly as she traced the outline of their figures with her fingertip.

Tears welled in her eyes, blurring the image before her. Memories of her mother flooded her heart. How she longed for the warmth of her mother's embrace, the sound of her laughter, the feeling of being loved unconditionally. The ache was a reminder of what was lost, of a void that had shaped her journey.

As the photograph slipped from her hand and back onto the dressing table, Hailey's reflection stared back at her from the mirror. All her life, she had fought to reclaim her sense of self, to rise above the darkness that had threatened to consume her.

But up until now, she just didn't know how.

Hailey's gaze wandered across the cardboard boxes stacked against the walls and a familiar sight caught her eye: her diary, a constant companion throughout her journey.

She carefully retrieved it from the box, feeling its weight in her hands. Its cover, worn and weathered, held the promise of pages filled with her thoughts, fears, and dreams.

With a sigh, Hailey settled onto the edge of her bed. The mattress felt foreign beneath her, as if it too sensed the impending changes. She placed the diary on her lap, its cover cool against her fingers. Opening it to a fresh page, she uncapped a pen and took a deep breath.

And began to write.

Diary entry:

It's funny how life keeps moving forward, even when it feels like my heart is stuck in the past. Today marks a year since I came to Mrs Wilson's home. A year of trying to rebuild, trying to heal, trying to find my place in the world. I guess some wounds take longer to heal than others.

I've been staring at these blank pages, wondering where to start. My head's a mess, and the words are tangled up in all the pain I've been trying so hard to ignore. I thought that coming here, leaving behind the past, would make everything better. But the truth is, the memories still haunt me.

The past seems to creep up when I least expect it. Their voices, their neglect, they all come back to me, even in my dreams. It's like I'm trapped in a never-ending loop, constantly fighting against the darkness.

Mrs Wilson has been kind, I'll give her that. She's tried to provide stability, to create a home where I can feel safe. And I appreciate it, I really do. But sometimes, when I'm alone in my room like I am now, I can't help but feel suffocated by the silence. The silence that brings back memories I wish I could forget.

I wish I could believe that I deserve happiness. That I'm not just some broken girl who's destined to be haunted by her past forever. But it's hard when every step I take feels like I'm walking on fragile ground, afraid that at any moment it will all crumble beneath me.

I want to trust again, to open my heart and let someone in. But the walls I've built are so high, and the scars are a constant reminder that people can hurt you, even when you least expect it. I know I should be moving forward, looking ahead to the new beginning that's waiting for me, but it's easier said than done.

Maybe one day I'll find the strength to let go of the pain, to let go of the past that's been holding me captive. Until then, I'll keep writing, keep trying to put these jumbled thoughts into words. Maybe one day these pages will hold more than just my sadness.

Chapter Five

Sasha stepped into the kitchen, worry tugging at her as she spotted Chloe in the buggy, tears streaming down her flushed cheeks. Without hesitation, she lifted the whimpering baby into her arms, feeling the warmth of the tiny body against her chest.

'Jesus, stop mollycoddling her, will you?'

Lindsay's sharp retort sliced through the air as she continued to apply her makeup, her irritation palpable. Her gaze briefly flickered to Josh, who sat on the sofa, cradling a cup of tea with the detachment of an observer in the midst of a brewing storm.

'Are you going to put these clothes away or do you think they're gonna do it themselves?' Her words dripped with resentment.

Josh promptly rose from his seat, exchanging a knowing look with Sasha, both well-acquainted with navigating Lindsay's moods.

'Are you still going out?' Sasha tried to redirect Lindsay's attention, sensing the escalating tension.

'For Christ's sake, yes! I need a break from this house and that screaming brat,' Lindsay snapped in frustration.

Sasha's gentle swaying continued, punctuated by occasional kisses on Chloe's head. 'She's not doing it deliberately, you know.'

'What the hell would you know, Sasha?' Lindsay's voice grew sharper. 'Are you suddenly an expert on parenting? No wonder you don't have any friends, Ms Know-It-All.'

Undeterred, Sasha held her ground, her voice steady. 'It's clear to anyone that Chloe's uncomfortable.'

'Then do something about it. Can't you see I'm trying to get ready?'

'When was her last dose of medicine?'

Lindsay's frown deepened. 'How am I supposed to remember?'

'Did you give it to her, though?'

'Ask your father. I'm swamped right now thinking about what the hell I'm going to tell my fans about the new book that I haven't even begun writing yet!'

Josh, starting to fold the laundry, said, 'I gave it to her an hour ago. It should start working soon.'

'That baby is all you seem to care about. To hell with my failing career and reputation.' Lindsay skilfully shifted gears, diverting the conversation and layering it with condescension. 'You're supposed to come with us tonight. My readers know I have an adult daughter, but they never see you. They probably think I'm hiding you out of embarrassment.'

Sasha swallowed the bitterness of her mother's words, recognising the insecurity that fuelled them. She stood firm, refusing to let the toxicity sway her.

'How about a glass of wine, darling?' Josh's gentle intervention aimed to ease the mounting tension and find a middle ground.

'I'd need the entire bottle, not a damn glass. Just pour me a brandy,' Lindsay shot back, her focus returning to Sasha. 'Both of you, get out of my sight. I need five bloody minutes of silence.'

Sasha seized the opportunity for escape. 'I'll take Chloe up to my room.'

'Before you go …' Lindsay snatched the brandy glass from Josh's hand. Sasha's heart sank, sensing impending drama in this interruption.

Lindsay took a gulp of her drink, her gaze intense as it locked onto Sasha.

'Changes are coming,' Lindsay declared, holding out her glass for a refill. 'We're hosting a guest. Hailey. She'll move in by the end of the week.'

Josh halted, surprised by the unexpected revelation. 'What? Shouldn't we have discussed this first?'

'Should've, could've, would've. You're hardly ever here to discuss anything,' Lindsay retorted dismissively.

Sasha's mind raced, grappling with the sudden news. A guest? How would this impact their already fragile family dynamic?

'Why would you agree to do something like that?' Josh dared to question.

'Because, my dear,' Lindsay retorted, 'it's called helping others. But I wouldn't expect you to grasp that concept. A schoolteacher's intellect, after all, isn't known for its brilliance.'

Sasha recognised a battle she couldn't win. When Lindsay's mind was set, resistance was futile.

'Have you even met her, Mum?'

'No, I haven't, Sasha,' Lindsay replied dismissively. 'But she's around your age. Just make sure you don't give off that weak vibe you got from your father.'

'How long will she be here?' Sasha said.

'Who knows?' Lindsay replied coldly. 'Depends on how useful she proves to be.'

A realisation struck Sasha like a blow: Her mother's motives weren't altruistic; they were calculated, transactional. It wasn't about compassion but necessity. Not that Sasha was surprised.

'I'm not sure this is a good idea, Lindsay,' Josh interjected. 'Especially if you don't know anything about her.'

Lindsay's eyes flashed with anger, her patience eroding. 'From what her dopey mentor said, she's had a turbulent life, bouncing between care homes. Makes your life look pretty cushy, doesn't it?' Lindsay sneered, throwing a glance in Sasha's direction. 'Maybe you can learn something from her.'

'Learn from a traumatised teen? I'm already one,' Sasha retorted, frustration overpowering her filter. She was done tiptoeing around her mother's temper.

'Are you really?' Lindsay's voice dripped with disdain. 'Maybe you need to attend one of those camps to learn respect, you ungrateful bitch. I hope your sister turns out to be better.'

Sasha's jaw clenched so tight it ached. She resisted the urge to engage, refusing to be baited into a futile argument. Holding Chloe tightly, she turned and left the room.

'Remember to prepare her formula the way your dad showed you,' Lindsay's voice trailed as Sasha ascended the stairs.

'Yes, Mum,' Sasha replied, her voice calm but devoid of genuine warmth.

Closing her bedroom door behind her, Sasha exhaled a sigh of relief when she heard the front door slam. The weight of her parents' presence seemed to lift with their departure. She walked over to the window, watching the red lights of their car fade into the darkness of the night.

Sitting on her bed, Sasha gently laid Chloe down, tucking her in with care. She leaned in and placed a tender kiss on Chloe's forehead.

'Just you and me, Chlo,' she whispered. 'One day, it'll be forever.'

For the first time that day, Sasha genuinely smiled, feeling a flicker of optimism amidst the chaos that surrounded her.

Chapter Six

The moon hung low in the indigo sky, casting its feeble light upon the desolate silhouette of the abandoned house. Hailey stood across the overgrown lawn, her heart aching as she stared at the place she once knew as home. A chilling breeze whispered through the trees, carrying with it a sense of melancholy that mirrored her own feelings.

In the silence of the night, Hailey's mind was a tumultuous sea of emotions. She couldn't comprehend why her biological parents had decided to put her into care, why she had been deemed unwanted and unworthy of love. Questions gnawed at her soul like relentless waves crashing against the shore. What had she done wrong? Was she not enough for her own parents to hold on to?

As Hailey approached the old house, her feet moving almost on autopilot, a cascade of memories flooded her senses. Echoes of screaming words of abuse, the rejection from her foster parents who had told her that their worst regret was fostering her. Hailey's whole horrid existence was etched into every corner of those walls. But now the walls stood bare, stripped of their former life, just like her heart.

Hailey stood before the weathered door, her hand trembling as she reached out to touch it. The wood was worn and splintered, much like the scars on her soul. This place, once called home, had been a battleground of pain and sorrow.

She took a deep breath, trying to steady herself, as she pushed the door open. The hinges creaked loudly, protesting the intrusion after years of abandonment. As she stepped inside, the musty smell of neglect assaulted her senses, mingling with the haunting memories of her past.

The dusty floorboards whispered under her feet as she moved through the desolate rooms. Broken fragments of a shattered mirror lay scattered on the floor, a reflection of the fractured life she had known here.

Hailey paused in what used to be her childhood bedroom. The walls, once adorned with colourful drawings and dreams, were now blank canvases mirroring the emptiness she felt inside. She couldn't help but remember the nights she had spent here, crying herself to sleep, desperate for love and acceptance that never came.

Outside, a gust of wind rattled the windows, causing her to shudder. It was as if the house itself mourned the pain it had witnessed, the echoes of her cries reverberating through the walls.

As she stood there, Hailey's heart found solace in the embrace of the abandoned house. In that desolate place, she realised that the answers she sought might never come, but her worth didn't have to be defined by the choices of others. She was not an abandoned house, left to decay; she was a soul, worthy of love and belonging, and the fact that she had been accepted by a new family was testament to that.

Chapter Seven

Upon arriving home, Sasha's gaze was immediately drawn to two unfamiliar cars parked beside her dad's. Curiosity mingled with resignation within her as she took in the sight. Their guest had arrived, another life set to intertwine with theirs. A sigh escaped her lips, finding solace in the hope that her mother would, for the time being, uphold her best behaviour.

Advancing up the path, the sound of laughter and her mother's voice reached her ears. Pushing open the front door, Sasha's eyes fell upon a teenager nestled between Lindsay and an unfamiliar woman on the sofa.

'Ah, Sasha, you're back. Come and say hello to Hailey.' Lindsay's voice held a rehearsed smile, which was etched onto her face.

Sasha's attention was captivated as she took in Hailey's presence. A stunning blend of beauty and mystery, Hailey's long dark hair framed delicate facial piercings. Dark, smudged eyeliner intensified the allure of her mesmerizing light blue eyes, reminiscent of the Caribbean Sea's vivid hue. Dressed in ripped jeans, black DM boots, and a plain black T-shirt, she exuded a rebellious charm.

Approaching the trio, Sasha extended her hand to Hailey. 'Nice to meet you, Hailey.'

'You too,' Hailey replied with a smile that carried a touch of mystery.

Sasha's gaze shifted to her father, apprehension evident in his eyes. She understood his unease; their family dynamics were strained, and the addition of a stranger only complicated matters.

'I've given Hailey the room next to yours, sweetheart.' Lindsay's words held a façade of enthusiasm.

Sasha's eyebrows shot up in surprise. Sweetheart? A term her mother never used with her. Aware of the charade, Sasha played along. 'That's great,' she responded, her tone neutral.

'Why don't we get a take-away tonight?' Lindsay turned her attention to Christine, a conspiratorial wink accompanying her suggestion. 'It's Hailey's first night here, and we wouldn't want to subject her to my cooking, no matter how "exquisite" it is.'

Suppressing the urge to point out her mother's culinary shortcomings, Sasha changed the subject. 'Where's Chloe?'

'She's napping for the afternoon.' Lindsay's voice carried a motherly warmth. 'You know how cranky she gets without enough sleep. Like mother, like daughter.'

Laughter briefly filled the air.

'Right, then!' Christine stood, signalling her departure. 'I'll leave you to settle in.'

Hailey rose, and the women shared a brief embrace.

'Don't be a stranger,' Christine said.

'I won't.'

'You'll see her plenty, Chris. You don't mind if

I call you Chris, do you?'

'Of course not. All my friends do.'

'Good.'

Sasha watched the wholesome scene unfold before her, a bittersweet ache tugging at her heart. *Why can't my mum be like this in real life?*

'I'll go and get the food, shall I?' Josh offered.

Lindsay nodded. 'Good idea.'

'Pizza all right with everyone?' Josh asked.

'Is it okay if I come with you?' Hailey turned to Josh. 'I'd like to ask if they've got any vacancies.'

'Of course.' Josh smiled, slipping on his jacket.

'That's a good idea. It'll probably do you good to meet new people,' Christine chimed in.

'Sasha? Are you coming?' Hailey turned her attention to Sasha, a hopeful expression in her eyes.

Sasha hesitated, briefly contemplating joining them. However, her concern for Chloe took precedence.

'Nah, I have some coursework to do, but you'll be back in no time. It's only around the corner.'

'It would be nice for you to get out for a bit, Sasha,' Lindsay encouraged, her tone gentle.

Sasha was resolute in her decision. 'I'm sure Dad and Hailey can manage. Right, Dad?' Her tone remained firm yet respectful.

'Of course,' Josh affirmed. 'Love, I'm taking your car, all right? Mine's already pulled in.'

'No problem, darling,' Lindsay replied with a touch of sweetness.

Hailey followed Josh towards the door, briefly

glancing back to give Sasha a small wave before disappearing from view.

Sasha could still feel the warmth of Hailey's hand on hers, and she discreetly caressed her palm with her fingertips as their voices gradually faded when the front door closed behind them.

Left alone in the house with Lindsay, Sasha felt a mixture of emotions stirring within her. She couldn't help but question why her family couldn't be like this in real life, why their interactions had to be filled with tension and resentment.

'Is there something in your eye?' Lindsay's tone dripped with sarcasm.

'No, I'm fine,' Sasha replied, her voice wavering slightly. She hadn't realised she was crying.

Lindsay reached over to Sasha and roughly swept her thumb over her cheek. 'Good. We don't want Hailey thinking you're a crybaby, now, do we? I can only hope that Chloe will grow up to be as lovely as her.'

'Yeah, in the same way Christine seems like the sort of loving mother any daughter would want.'

Lindsay snarled, ready to unleash her wrath upon Sasha, but before she could, Sasha swiftly made her escape, hurrying out of the room and upstairs to check on Chloe. The sight of her little sister peacefully sleeping in her cot brought a sense of relief to Sasha. She stayed by Chloe's side, watching over her until she heard Josh and Hailey burst through the front door, their voices filled with excitement and chatter. Reluctantly, she went back downstairs to join them.

'I'll just freshen up if that's okay?' Hailey said.

'Of course,' Lindsay said, smiling sweetly.

As soon as Hailey was out of earshot, Lindsay grabbed Josh roughly by his arm. 'Where the hell have you been? I'm starving while you're out having a good time!'

Josh yanked his arm out from her grip. 'We couldn't get pizza. They were closed, so we had to look for something else.'

'Where? Edinburgh?' Lindsay spat.

'No, we drove to Windmill Street,' Josh said as he lifted the bag of food he held in his hand.

'They're coming in three weeks, Josh!' Hailey said excitedly as she burst into the kitchen. 'Wembley!'

'I'll get us tickets. Check the dates!' Josh exclaimed, a wide grin spreading across his face.

Curiosity piqued, Lindsay's eyes narrowed. 'Tickets for what?'

'We heard Iron Maiden's on tour on the radio. You know I'm a big fan. Turns out Hailey grew up on their later stuff. How and when did I get this old?' Josh laughed to himself as he unpacked the food, the tantalising aroma filling the room.

'Don't you think you're a little too old for that kind of thing?' Lindsay delivered the words bluntly, a subtle reminder that Josh was stepping out of line.

'No!' Josh said. 'It'll be a great experience. I'm sure Sasha will love it too.'

'And what about me?' Lindsay asked, her hand resting on her hip.

He looked at her with mild ridicule, his face contorted in disbelief. 'You?'

'Yes, me,' Lindsay said.

'You listen to Josh Groban and Celine Dion, Lindsay. You would hate it,' Josh retorted.

'You can't go to a concert with two teenagers, Josh. One of them could get lost in such a big crowd,' Lindsay warned.

But Sasha could see beyond her mother's words. It wasn't really about anyone's safety; it was about Lindsay's jealousy, her fear of losing Josh's attention to someone else, especially to a woman half his age.

In that moment, Sasha realised that Hailey's presence was not going to improve things in the Miller house after all. It was only going to make things worse.

Chapter Eight

Lying in the soft embrace of her new bed, Hailey felt a sense of peace wash over her. The day had been a whirlwind of emotions, and now, as the moonlight filtered through the curtains, she had a chance to reflect on the experience. Her new bedroom left her in awe; even though she knew it wasn't her permanent home, she was grateful to be lying in her very first double bed. It was a luxury she had never experienced before, and she marvelled at the fact that she could sprawl out without her legs dangling over a creaky wooden bedframe, which had often given her numerous bruises. But what she appreciated even more was the newfound sense of privacy. In her previous foster home, the other residents seemed to think nothing of barging into her room without knocking or rummaging through her belongings when she wasn't there.

Another positive was a certain somebody.

From the moment she had laid eyes on Sasha, Hailey had taken an instant liking to her. Sasha had extended a warm and genuine welcome, making Hailey feel like an old friend rather than a stranger. The entire family had embraced her, creating an environment that felt more like a loving family than just a temporary shelter.

So far, all she knew about Sasha was that she was studying at a local university, which had surprised her at first. People their age were normally keen to venture into the unknown and move away from the city they were born in, but Hailey knew she was generalising. It was evident that Sasha had a very close bond with her baby sister, Chloe, so that was reason enough to stay close to home.

Hailey bolted upright at the sound of a tap on the door. Her eyes fell on the clock. Eleven p.m. Her first thought was that something was wrong, and she immediately jumped out of bed and went to the door. Pulling it back, she was surprised to see Lindsay standing there with a mug of what smelled like hot chocolate in her hand.

'I hope I didn't wake you,' Lindsay said in a hushed voice.

'No.'

'Good. I just thought you'd be feeling a little unsettled, so I brought you a hot chocolate to help you get some sleep. It always helped with Sasha.'

'Thank you, that's really kind of you.' Hailey took the cup. 'Night, then.'

As she attempted to close the door, Lindsay gently pushed back against it.

'Do you mind if I sit with you while you drink it?' Lindsay asked.

While Hailey thought it an odd request, she nodded in agreement and climbed back into bed as Lindsay closed the door.

Lindsay took a seat in the chair by the window. 'I hope your bed is comfortable enough. It's a memory foam mattress.'

Hailey took a sip of the sweet liquid and nodded. 'It feels like heaven.'

Lindsay gave a sad smile. 'Good. I suppose you didn't have many luxuries growing up?'

'Not really.'

Lindsay leaned back in the chair, her expression thoughtful. 'Would you mind telling me a bit about your past? I mean, only if you're comfortable. I don't know if Christine told you, but I write parenting books.'

Hailey's gaze met Lindsay's, and she found herself nodding slowly. 'Yeah, she did. If only more parents were aware of what having kids entailed before having them, there would be less children abandoned.'

Lindsay's gaze remained steady, her eyes reflecting both understanding and sadness. 'You're right. I'll admit I wasn't the perfect mother when I had Sasha, but through trial and error, I learned to be the best supportive mother I could be.'

Lindsay's admission wasn't what she had expected. 'Your kids are lucky to have you.'

A smile tugged at the corners of Lindsay's lips. 'No, I'm lucky to have them. I don't know what I would do without them. And now, having you here is the icing on the cake.'

Hailey hesitated, her fingers tracing the rim of the cup. 'Thanks.'

'I mean it. So, how old were you when you entered the system?' Lindsay's voice was kind, inviting.

'Well, the first time, I was a baby. I was adopted,

but Maggie died when I was seven. I then went to foster parents for a few years, but my foster mother ended up taking me to a meeting with a social worker one day and just leaving me there.'

'What!?'

'Yeah, I didn't even realise she wasn't coming back until they took me to another foster home.'

'That's a terrible thing to do. What was it like being in foster homes, generally?'

'They were … okay, I s'pose. Some were better than others. But it always felt temporary, you know? Like I was just passing through.'

'Did you ever feel truly cared for in any of them?'

Hailey closed her eyes, memories resurfacing. 'There were a couple where it felt like they genuinely cared. But it's complicated. Every time I started to get close to a family, it felt like they would give up on me, or I'd get moved to a new home. So, I learned to keep people at arm's length, to not let myself get too attached.'

'And what about friends?' Lindsay's tone held a hint of understanding. 'Did you make any?'

Hailey's lips curved into a bittersweet smile. 'I tried. But people come and go so quickly in foster care. It's hard to make proper friends. I mean, I wasn't the only child there. There were a few of us. We used to call ourselves the unwantables, and I s'pose that's how I feel even up until today.'

'The unwantables,' Lindsay repeated quietly to herself. 'I can only imagine how tough that must have been for you. Did you ever have a sense of stability, a place where you felt like you belong?'

Hailey's gaze met Lindsay's, and for a moment, the weight of her past seemed to lessen. 'Not really. Until now, I guess.'

'Hailey,' Lindsay said, her voice gentle but firm, 'please know that you are deserving of love and care, and your worth as a person is not determined by the past. Your biological mother's decision was influenced by circumstances you may never know, but it's not a reflection of your value as a human being.'

Hearing these words, though familiar, still struck a raw nerve, tearing at the wounds that had never quite healed.

Hailey nodded in understanding.

'Just know that you're here now, and I hope you know that you're part of this family too.'

A tear escaped Hailey's eye and she hastily wiped it away. Sharing her past had felt both daunting and freeing.

'Thanks. It means a lot.'

'Any time you want to share, I'm here.'

It was a simple promise, yet it held a world of possibility. Maybe, in this house, with this family, she really could find a new beginning.

Chapter Nine

Sasha's mind wandered away from the tutorial, caught up in thoughts of the late-night conversation she'd heard between her mother and Hailey. The idea of eavesdropping had crossed her mind, but fatigue had taken over, and she'd dozed off, only waking up when Chloe's five a.m. cries broke the silence.

It wasn't until her name was called that she snapped back to the present.

'Sasha, care to share your thoughts on the topic?' Dr Anderson's enquiry pierced through the haze, casting a spotlight on Sasha, who blinked rapidly when she found herself the centre of attention.

Caught off guard and feeling a bit embarrassed, Sasha stumbled over her words. 'Um, I'm sorry, could you repeat the question?'

'I asked you about technology's impact on the travel industry and how it has changed the way people plan and experience trips.'

'Oh, right! Well, you know, these days, you can pretty much plan an entire trip with just a few clicks on your computer or phone. There are tons of websites and apps to help you find the best flights and hotels. And let's not forget about social media! People share their travel stories all over Instagram and Facebook, giving you loads of ideas and tips for your own adventure. It's like carrying a virtual tour guide in your pocket.'

Dr Anderson gave a nod of approval and the discussion continued with Sasha's mind circling back to her mother and Hailey. She was determined to unravel the mystery of their late-night conversation, but she knew she had to be strategic.

I'll need to find a time to chat with Hailey when my mum isn't hanging around. Something's definitely up.

After her last lecture, Sasha headed towards the exit. Lost in her thoughts, she was startled when she heard a familiar voice calling out to her.

'Hey, Sasha! Wait up!'

Butterflies stirred in her stomach. It was Hailey.

Oh my god. What is she doing here? Is she lost?

Hailey caught up with her, and Sasha attempted to sound casual.

'Hey, I didn't expect to see you here.'

'I was in town and remembered you mentioning you come here. Mind if I walk home with you?'

'Nope, glad of the company.'

As they walked along the street, Sasha realised that she had hardly thought about Dr Anderson all day; her attention had been solely on Hailey. Could it be real? Could she actually be developing feelings for Hailey? Glancing sideways, she saw Hailey gazing at her with an intensity that seemed to mirror her own internal struggle. Did Hailey feel the same way?

Don't be stupid. Of course she doesn't. What the hell would she see in someone like me?

'So, what are you studying?'

'Travel and tourism.'

Hailey laughed. 'Really? You know how awful tourists can be, right? If you make a mistake with their tickets, they'll bitch and whine at you all day. I know. I've seen it when I worked part-time in a travel agent.'

'How do you know I'm not taking this course to be a tour guide?' Sasha said, her hands seeking warmth between her pockets.

'A tour guide is even worse! Same tourists, but you're responsible for your entire group's safety and have to answer all their questions. You deal with some real arseholes,' Hailey explained. 'Who wants to travel abroad anyway?'

Sasha came to an abrupt stop, causing Hailey to do the same.

'I do. The world's an amazing place, and I want to explore it all! I'm planning on giving tours in every corner of the planet before I turn eighty. After that, my dream is to live in a cosy cottage, surrounded by a bunch of animals.'

Hailey stared at her, her expression intense.

'Why are you looking at me like that?'

'No reason. I'm just listening,' Hailey said. 'Your ambitions, your belief that there's this whole exciting world out there … it's kind of inspiring.'

Sasha arched an eyebrow. 'Are you being sarcastic?'

'Not at all! I mean it. I've never really had reasons for plans or goals. You, on the other hand, make it seem like nothing's impossible.'

'You don't have dreams?' Sasha asked, genuinely

surprised. The idea of not having aspirations was foreign to her. 'How can someone like you not want to move forward in life?'

'Someone like me …'

'Yeah! You're so beautiful, you can do anything you want,' Sasha blurted out, not realising that she was speaking her thoughts aloud.

Hailey's gaze lingered on Sasha with a look she couldn't quite decipher.

'You really think I'm beautiful?' Hailey smiled.

Sasha nodded hesitantly, still feeling a bit awkward for expressing her feelings so openly. But to her surprise, Hailey seemed genuinely appreciative.

'Coming from you, that means a lot,' Hailey said, giving Sasha a playful wink. 'You're beautiful too, even if you do try to hide it by keeping your head down most of the time.'

The observation caught Sasha off guard. She wasn't accustomed to receiving compliments, especially not from someone as stunning and confident as Hailey. She blushed, feeling a mixture of flattery and unease. Wanting to shift the focus away from herself, Sasha quickly changed the subject.

'Do you think you'll go to university?'

'I've thought about it.'

'What would you study if you did?'

'Sports science,' Hailey said. 'I'll let you in on a little secret: I have a fascination with human anatomy.'

'Cool. So why didn't you apply to attend this year?'

Hailey's expression darkened, but she quickly composed herself before responding. 'Life's different when you've got no one in your corner. You're lucky to have such great parents who support you and want the best for you.'

Sasha was about to inform Hailey the person who had encouraged her to go to university was her Aunt Jo, that her parents had actively tried to discourage her – her mum especially – but decided against it. Who was she to shatter Hailey's illusion of her dysfunctional family?

If she hangs around long enough, she'll find out for herself.

'Oh, I was gonna ask you about last night. I heard you and my mum talking. I hope she wasn't bothering you.'

'Not at all. She was really sweet, actually.'

Sweet is one word I would not describe my mum as.

'Oh right, as long as she wasn't going on about her parenting skills.'

Hailey laughed. 'No, she was asking about my life.'

'Sorry, I—'

'There's nothing to apologise for. I really didn't mind.'

They walked in silence for a few moments, until Sasha turned to Hailey.

'Do you mind me asking something personal?'

'Go for it.'

'Do you miss your mum? I mean, your real one.'

'I never knew her.' Hailey's voice held a matter-of-fact tone. 'And anyway, she didn't care about me when she gave me up, so why should I miss her?'

Sasha instinctively covered her mouth, a wave of remorse washing over her for broaching such a sensitive topic. However, Hailey's demeanour remained detached, a level of emotional distance that was hard for Sasha to fully grasp.

'My mum could be dead for all I know,' Hailey continued, her words carrying a similar detached air.

Sasha wanted to comfort her, but Hailey's demeanour didn't invite sympathy.

'The thought of being alone in this world is horrible, Hailey. I can't even begin to imagine how hard it's been for you.'

'I hope you never have to,' Hailey replied softly.

Sasha held Hailey's gaze, sensing a connection that transcended their disparate pasts. Each carried their own set of scars, some visible and others hidden beneath the surface.

Out of the blue, Hailey linked her arm with Sasha's. 'All right, enough of the heavy stuff. I'm here to get to know you.'

As they strolled side by side, Sasha couldn't shake the notion that this burgeoning friendship held profound potential, a promise of shared exploration and mutual understanding. If only she could summon the bravery to confront the unspoken truths nestled within her own heart.

Chapter Ten

Sasha had always been the kind of person who believed she could handle anything on her own. But as she stared at the diagram of global travel routes and tourism trends on her computer screen, a sense of overwhelm crept in. The assignment, a pivotal part of her university course, was much more challenging than she had anticipated. She sighed and raked her fingers through her hair. At that moment her phone pinged.

Hey, how's it going? Haven't seen you today. You hiding from me?

LOL! No, but I wish I could hide from this project!!!'

What's up? You need help?

Sasha hesitated for a moment, then typed out her reply:

I could actually. That's if you don't mind?

She waited for a reply but none came. Instead, there was a tap on her door.
'Come in.'
The door opened and there stood Hailey, smiling

at her. 'See the benefits of living next door to one another.'

Sasha laughed.

'Right,' Hailey said, crossing the room and sitting next to her on the bed. 'What's the problem?'

Sasha bit her lip. 'I'm stuck on a question about analysing global travel patterns. It's way more difficult than I thought.'

'I'm pretty good with data analysis. Let's see if we can figure it out together.'

Sasha stole a quick glance at Hailey, and she couldn't help but feel a jolt of excitement as she leaned in to look at the question. Her presence was reassuring, and as she focused on the task at hand, Sasha found herself drawn to her even more – her confidence, her intelligence … *her body!*

'Are you okay?' Hailey's voice broke through her reverie.

Sasha blinked, her cheeks warming as she realised she had been staring. 'Oh, um, yeah. Just lost in thought for a moment.'

'Happens to the best of us. You're right, this question is a bit tricky,' Hailey said, studying the data on the screen again. 'Okay, I think I see the issue. We need to break this down into smaller segments and analyse each region's travel trends individually.'

'Sounds like a plan.'

As Hailey began outlining her idea on a notepad, Sasha found herself captivated. Hailey made it seem so simple, so manageable.

Over the next couple of hours, Hailey and Sasha

worked side by side, poring over the data, debating different approaches, and gradually piecing together the puzzle. The close proximity between them was becoming increasingly apparent, and Sasha couldn't ignore the flutter in her stomach every time their arms brushed or their hands accidentally touched. Hailey's presence was intoxicating, and she had to remind herself several times not to stare.

'Wow, I can't believe we actually cracked it,' Sasha said, a sense of amazement in her voice.

Hailey grinned. 'Right? We make a great team.'

In more ways than one.

Sasha's thoughts drifted to the growing connection she felt with Hailey. It wasn't just about the project; it was about the chemistry between them, the shared moments, the way Hailey understood her without words.

Sasha realised her feelings were quickly evolving into something deeper. Hailey wasn't just a friend; she was becoming a lifeline, a source of comfort and support that she hadn't realised she needed. And as they exchanged a smile, she knew that this was only the beginning of a journey that held the promise of something truly special.

Chapter Eleven

'Mm, something smells good,' Hailey said as she walked into the kitchen with Sasha.

Lindsay turned around and eyed them both. Hailey thought again how attractive Lindsay was. Most of the women she'd encountered around her age didn't look after themselves the way Lindsay seemed to, which was a feat in itself considering how busy she was as an author, mother, and wife. Hailey still couldn't get her head around Lindsay opening her house to a complete stranger. This spoke volumes about the kind of woman she was.

Hailey took in the numerous pots on the hob with raised eyebrows. 'You must have been cooking all day.'

A fleeting look of confusion flickered across Lindsay's face, quickly replaced by a smile that didn't quite reach her eyes.

'Yes, you could definitely say that. Can you cook?'

'Yeah, but not the fancy dishes you see on TV. I'd love to be able to create those,' Hailey said.

'Well, I'm more than willing to be your taste tester. Someone has to enjoy all those incredible dishes you'll be whipping up,' Sasha said.

Hailey laughed. 'You're on. I'll hold you to that.'

Hailey hurried over to Lindsay's side to assist in

arranging the plates on the dining table.

'Your family must be so grateful for everything you do.'

Lindsay let out a dry laugh, her eyes glinting with an almost cynical amusement. 'It's a mother's job to care for the family. Anyway, enough about me and all the hard work I do. Let's enjoy our first home-cooked meal together.'

She gestured for Hailey and Sasha to take a seat.

The door opened and Josh walked in carrying a bottle of wine, seemingly preoccupied with his own thoughts.

'I hope I've cooked the chicken enough; I know—' Josh began, only to halt abruptly as he noticed Hailey and Sasha seated at the table. 'Oh, I didn't hear you both come in.'

A subtle change in the room's atmosphere suddenly became noticeable. Lindsay's forced cheerfulness now seemed more transparent. Josh appeared uneasy, his fingers stumbling over the wine bottle opener as he searched for words.

'Here you go, darling,' Josh said, his tone almost too bright as he poured two glasses and sat down. 'Right, let's dig in, shall we?'

Hailey felt a pang of jealousy shoot through her. Not because she was envious of Josh and Lindsay as a couple, more so because she had never had anyone treat her with such thoughtfulness.

She savoured a bite of the succulent roasted chicken, its golden skin glistening with a tempting crispness.

'This tastes as delicious as it looks, Lindsay,' Hailey said.

'If luck's on your side, maybe one day I'll share my secret recipe with you,' Lindsay said.

'That'd be fantastic.'

As the meal continued, moments of awkward silence punctuated the clinking of cutlery and glasses.

'Sasha, do you fancy going to the cinema tonight? My treat,' Hailey said.

'And what about Chloe?' Lindsay replied before Sasha had a chance to.

Hailey laughed. 'I don't think babies are allowed into eighteen-rated films.'

Within a matter of seconds, Hailey's laughter dimmed as she observed the intensity of Lindsay's gaze on Sasha.

'Sasha normally puts Chloe to sleep, don't you, sweetheart? It's the only time the two sisters get to bond.' Lindsay turned to Hailey. 'You didn't grow up with a real family, so you wouldn't quite understand.'

Lindsay's words carried a bitterness that couldn't be ignored, as if her comment was laced with venom – more of a deliberate barb than a mere explanation.

Hailey shared a surprised glance with Sasha, who appeared taken aback and slightly embarrassed.

Hailey took a deep breath, determined not to let Lindsay's words get under her skin.

'You're right, Lindsay. I didn't grow up with a real family as you put it,' Hailey responded calmly. 'So what would I know?'

'I didn't mean to imply anything.' Lindsay's tone softened. 'It's just … being a mother can be overwhelming, and sometimes it's hard to see past our own struggles.'

'I seem to have lost my appetite. I think I'll have an early night if that's okay.' Hailey pushed her chair back and stood. 'We can go to the cinema on Saturday afternoon if you like.'

'I—' Sasha's response was cut short.

'Unfortunately, Sasha will be on babysitting duty all weekend. I'm beginning work on my new book, and I need some uninterrupted time to gather my thoughts.'

'All right, well, I guess I'll see you all tomorrow. Have a good night.'

Hailey's departure was met with an awkward silence. She sensed the weight of Lindsay's gaze on her as she made her way across the room.

'I'll come with you,' Sasha said, quickly following Hailey to the door.

As they stepped into the hallway, Sasha gently caught Hailey's arm, turning her around. Her eyes held a sincere apology.

'I'm really sorry about my mum. She can be a bit insensitive sometimes,' Sasha whispered.

'It's not your fault, and she's right, I didn't grow up with my real family,' Hailey replied, offering a small smile. 'Seriously, I'm fine. I just need some fresh air.'

Hailey appreciated Sasha's support, but she could sense her internal struggle between staying with her and returning to the kitchen.

'And as for Saturday, let's take Chloe to the cinema with us. I'm sure there'll be something suitable for her.'

'Are you sure?'

'Positive. Now go on, go eat your dinner before it gets cold.'

Sasha returned to the kitchen and Hailey stepped outside into the tranquil night. The quiet street provided a space for reflection on the unexpected tension of the evening.

Lindsay's comment had got under her skin, more than she cared to admit. But she remembered something she had learnt back at the residential camp she'd attended: *I can't control what others say or do, but I sure as hell can decide how I'm gonna react.*

She decided to take Sasha's tip about her mum being insensitive and leave it at that.

Maybe it's me being overly sensitive. If I'm going to fit into this family, I've got to remember Lindsay is not like my foster mother. I'm going to have to stop being so easily triggered.

However, even as she thought this, Hailey realised it would be a tougher task than anticipated. The wounds from her past were deep-rooted and shaking off years of emotional scars proved challenging. She had spent so long guarding herself from the pain, that opening up to a new family sometimes felt like she was constantly walking on a tightrope.

She only hoped she wouldn't lose her balance.

Later that night, in bed, she opened her diary.

Diary entry:

What a day! Sometimes, life takes unexpected turns, and today was a whirlwind of emotions that's left me confused. I really enjoy spending time with Sasha. She has this genuine warmth that draws you in, making me feel like I've known her for much longer than I have. The way she talks about her dreams and goals, the enthusiasm she has for life, it's really inspiring. I can't deny that there's a part of me that's genuinely excited to get to know her better. And I can't shake off the feeling that maybe, just maybe, she feels the same way about me.

We've chatted about so many things over the last couple of days – our aspirations, our experiences, even our families. She's got this ability to make me wanna open up, to share things I haven't spoken about in a long time. I can't help but feel a sense of comfort around her, like I can just be myself.

Just the way she talks about everything. I'm standing there, thinking, 'Wow, this girl knows how to live'. And those moments, those glances, those smiles – they're like secret messages only we understand.

But I can't help but wonder if I'm reading too much into it. What if I'm misinterpreting her friendliness for something more? What if this whole connection is just a one-sided fantasy? It's like I'm standing on the edge of a cliff, and the fall could be amazing or disastrous.

Risking our friendship is a big deal. What if my feelings mess things up? What if she doesn't feel the same way and things get awkward?

Still, there's this tiny voice inside me saying, 'Go for it'. Life's all about taking risks, right? And there's something about Sasha that's worth the gamble. It's not just about romantic feelings; it's about finding someone who gets you.

Maybe I'm getting ahead of myself. Maybe I should just let things unfold naturally. Maybe I'm just reading too much into those shared moments, and Sasha's just being a great friend. Ugh, why does my mind have to overanalyse everything?

Anyway, tomorrow's a new day. Who knows what adventures – or misadventures – await? I guess the universe has its way of guiding us, even if we're stumbling through the dark.

PS. Lindsay's behaviour was a bit off today. Too early to know if I'm reading too much into it or not!!!

I MUST NOT REACT!!!!!!

Chapter Twelve

Even after eighteen years, Lindsay's knack for leaving Sasha dumbfounded had not waned – in fact, it seemed to have grown stronger, and always in the most unfavourable way. Throughout the meal, Sasha had diligently maintained a façade of composure, masking her annoyance beneath a practised smile. Yet, despite her best efforts, she found herself unable to shake off the impact of Lindsay's cutting comment. It was as if Lindsay possessed an uncanny ability to locate and exploit the chinks in somebody's emotional armour, leaving them feeling exposed and vulnerable. Her comment to Hailey had been delivered with a casualness that belied its potency, a perfectly aimed arrow that found its mark with unerring accuracy. And now, long after the words had been spoken, they continued to reverberate within Sasha's mind, each repetition driving the barb deeper.

Walking into Lindsay's office with clenched fists, Sasha had to use every ounce of mental strength not to lose her temper. 'Why did you have to be so mean to Hailey?'

'I have no idea what you're talking about,' Lindsay replied, her fingers busily tapping away on her laptop.

'Really? The family bond thing wasn't a dig at Hailey because she had the nerve to ask me to go out and have fun?' Sasha said, folding her arms across her chest.

Lindsay let out an exaggerated yawn and turned around in her seat, her dismissive demeanour evident. 'You really do overthink too much. It's one of your many bad traits that I despise.'

'Seriously, why did you bring Hailey here to live with us?'

Lindsay stood up, giving Sasha a sickly sweet smile. 'Why? Because I'm a good person.'

Hearing Chloe crying in the background, Lindsay's mood shifted in an instant, her anger boiling to the surface. 'Now can you go and settle that bloody baby down before I scream. I'm on a roll with my writing at the moment.'

'At least something good is happening in your life. You know what? I hope Hailey see's you for what you are and packs up and leaves.'

Sasha walked to the door before stopping, her hand gripping the handle. 'Oh, and when Dad gets back, tell him I really enjoyed the meal he made tonight.'

Sasha tiptoed into the nursery. The soft glow of a nightlight cast a warm, gentle ambience. Chloe, wrapped in a soft blanket, lay peacefully in the crib, little hands clutching onto a plush teddy bear.

'Hey there, little one,' Sasha whispered, her voice filled with tenderness. 'Time for bed, huh?'

She carefully picked up Chloe, cradling her in her arms. As she rocked gently back and forth, she softly hummed a lullaby, the familiar tune wrapping the room in a cocoon of comfort.

Chloe's eyes blinked sleepily, her tiny fingers

curling around Sasha's shirt. Sasha smiled down at her, her heart melting at the sight of the little bundle in her arms.

'Shh, it's okay,' Sasha whispered, stroking Chloe's silky hair. 'I'm here, and I'll keep you safe.'

She continued to sway, the rhythm soothing both Chloe and herself. Sasha had always found peace in the quiet moments of the night, and now, cradling this precious life in her arms, she felt a sense of purpose and warmth fill her heart.

With a gentle kiss on her forehead, Sasha laid Chloe back down in the cot, making sure she was comfortable and secure. She softly caressed Chloe's cheek one last time before slipping out of the nursery, leaving the door slightly ajar.

Sasha got ready for bed. Although it was late, she was restless. Every time she closed her eyes, she recalled Hailey's hurt expression at the dinner table earlier that evening. The memory tugged at her heartstrings, and she wished she could have done something to make it go away, to erase the pain that lingered in Hailey's eyes.

When she heard a noise coming from Hailey's room, she lay motionless for a moment, listening intently. There it was again, barely audible, but enough for her to recognise what it was. A muffled sob.

Worried, Sasha slipped out of bed, pulling on her dressing gown. She crossed the hallway, her footsteps barely making a sound on the creaky floorboards. As she approached Hailey's room, the sound of her sobs grew louder. Sasha pushed the door open gently and saw

Hailey lying on her side, her face crumpled in distress even in her sleep.

Carefully, Sasha approached the bed and sat down next to Hailey, the moonlight filtering through the curtains, casting a soft glow on her tear-stained cheeks. Sasha's heart ached at the sight of Hailey's vulnerability.

She placed her hand on Hailey's trembling shoulder.

'Hailey,' she whispered, 'it's okay. You're safe.'

Hailey stirred, her eyes fluttering open. Confusion flickered in her gaze before she registered Sasha's presence.

'Sasha?' she whispered; her voice choked with emotion.

'I heard you crying,' Sasha said softly. 'What's wrong?'

Hailey buried her face in her hands as she struggled to find the words. 'I … I miss having my own family,' she said, her voice breaking.

Sasha's heart swelled with empathy. Without a second thought, she climbed into the bed, wrapping her arms around Hailey and pulling her close. Her tears dampened Sasha's nightshirt, but she didn't mind.

'Shh, it's okay,' Sasha murmured, her voice soothing. 'I'm here for you.'

Hailey sniffled. 'Is your mum angry with me for spoiling dinner?'

'What! No. You didn't spoil anything, Hailey. If anyone's responsible, it's my mother. She had no right to speak to you like that.'

I can handle what my mother does to me but when I see her hurt someone else, I could … Sasha's thoughts trailed off. She didn't want to go there. Didn't want to hear the words she thought almost every day. That she wished her mother would simply disappear from their lives and never come back.

She knew Hailey would probably be shocked if she heard her inner thoughts, but that's all they were, thoughts, and she had no intention of sharing them with anyone.

'I know but I don't want to rock the boat. I've only been here two days and I already feel like I've messed up.'

My mother is a fucking genius. I don't know how she does it, but she always seems to make herself look like the victim.

Sasha gave Hailey a reassuring squeeze. 'I promise you've done nothing wrong. You've got nothing to worry about.'

Hailey's eyes brimmed with emotion.

'Thank you,' she said softly. 'I'm so lucky to have you as my friend.'

Without a word, Sasha gently brushed a tear from Hailey's cheek. Hailey's eyes met hers, and in that fleeting moment, a silent understanding passed between them.

'I never thought I could trust anyone like this,' Hailey whispered, her voice barely audible.

'You can trust me, Hailey. I'm here for you, no matter what.'

Hailey's hand reached out and found Sasha's

fingers, entwining them with her own, as if they were two puzzle pieces meant to fit together.

They lay there in silence, only the soft sound of Hailey's sniffling breaking the stillness of the night. Sasha rocked Hailey gently, just as she would soothe Chloe while she cried. The rhythmic motion, the warmth of Sasha's embrace, seemed to offer a sense of security that Hailey desperately needed.

Once Hailey had fallen asleep, Sasha tucked her in, lingering for a moment before she quietly made her way back to her own room.

***

Sunrays cast a warm glow through the kitchen windows as Sasha stood in front of the hob, preparing breakfast. Chloe, happily seated in the high chair, giggled while playing with her toy.

Sasha stirred the eggs and turned at the sound of approaching footsteps. Hailey entered, looking somewhat embarrassed. Their eyes met, the memory of the previous night still fresh.

'Hey,' Hailey mumbled, her cheeks tinted with a blush.

'Hey,' Sasha said, placing the spatula down. 'Did you sleep through the night?'

'Yeah,' Hailey said, averting her gaze.

Sasha resumed cooking, and Hailey settled into a chair at the kitchen table, observing Sasha's graceful movements as she juggled various tasks.

'I hope you're a fan of scrambled eggs, bacon, and avocado,' Sasha said.

'Sounds good.'

'So, any plans for today?'

'Yeah, I'll be job hunting.'

'Good luck.'

'Thanks, I'll need it.'

'Don't worry, you'll do great.'

A loud knock echoed from the front door. Sasha wiped her hands on a kitchen towel before making her way to the hallway. As she opened the door, a deliveryman stood there, holding a package.

'Delivery for Hailey Summers,' he announced cheerfully. 'Here you go.'

'Thanks,' Sasha said. After signing for the package, she closed the door and returned to the kitchen.

She placed the package in front of Hailey, who looked genuinely surprised.

'That's for me?'

'Yep.'

'But no one knows I'm here.'

'Someone does.'

As Hailey examined the package, Lindsay walked into the kitchen. Her gaze shifted from Hailey to the package and back again.

'Oh, I ordered you a new mobile phone,' Lindsay stated casually, as if it were the most ordinary thing in the world.

Hailey's eyes widened in astonishment. 'You got me a phone?'

'Yeah, well, I noticed your old one was falling apart. Thought an upgrade would be nice,' Lindsay explained with a shrug.

'Thank you so much, Lindsay,' Hailey exclaimed gratefully. 'You really didn't need to do that.'

Lindsay waved off Hailey's appreciation. 'Consider it an apology. Sasha was right, I shouldn't have made that remark yesterday,' she said. 'Here, let me take it. I'll need to set the sim up for you from my account.'

Hailey passed Lindsay the box.

Sasha observed the interaction in silence, a slight unease settling at the back of her mind. Lindsay's reputation for self-centeredness and her reluctance to spend money on others, especially in the form of gifts, raised a red flag.

What could have prompted Lindsay's sudden display of generosity?

Sasha observed Lindsay closely. Her body language seemed slightly guarded, as if she were hiding something. Sasha's instincts told her that there was more to this generous act than met the eye.

However, she didn't want to spoil the mood, especially when Hailey seemed so happy about her new phone. So, Sasha decided to ignore her reservations – for now anyway.

'Just to let you know, I'm going out on Sunday, Mum,' Sasha said.

Sasha noticed a quick spark of anger flicker across Lindsay's eyes.

'I don't remember us discussing this,' Lindsay

retorted, a hint of irritation lacing her words.

'I'm going to Aunt Jo's.'

Hailey gave her an enquiring look and Sasha offered a brief explanation. 'Aunt Jo is my dad's older sister. I promised to pick up some clothes she's got for the charity shop.'

'I hope you're not going to be back too late,' Lindsay said with a tight smile.

'Probably about nine,' Sasha said. 'I'm staying for dinner. I wrote it on the calendar two weeks ago. I thought you'd seen it.'

The difference between Lindsay and Jo never ceased to amaze Sasha. They seemed like two sides of a coin, each possessing entirely different traits and personalities. While Lindsay was aloof and detached, Jo was warm and inviting, and Jo's sincere interest in Sasha's life made her feel cherished, a stark contrast to the distant demeanour of her own mother.

'I'd like to meet her someday if that's okay,' Hailey said.

'Definitely. You'll love her, she's great.'

'Hadn't you better get a move on? I don't want Chloe to be late for nursery,' Lindsay interjected, a touch of impatience in her voice.

'Oh, I didn't know Chloe went to nursery. I can take her if you like,' Hailey offered.

'No, I don't want to disrupt her routine,' Lindsay replied.

Her calm, smooth voice immediately set off alarm bells in Sasha's mind. Over the years, she had learned to recognize that tone – it was the façade Lindsay used to mask her true emotions. Behind that polished exterior, Sasha knew there was often a storm brewing.

Breakfast was eaten in silence, and after putting the dishes away, Hailey slipped into her jacket.

'I'm off, then. I'll see you later.'

Once Hailey left, Sasha prepared herself for what she knew was coming next.

'I did not give you permission to go anywhere on Sunday.' The calm of Lindsay's voice had been replaced with one of fury. 'Do you think you're safe because you've made a little friend? Well, think again. As long as you're under my roof, you'll abide by my rules.'

'And what're they? To provide free childcare?'

The room fell silent for a moment as their eyes locked in a battle of wills. But Lindsay's smirk revealed her satisfaction at having the upper hand.

'If you don't like it, you know what you can do. Pack your bags and get the fuck out of here,' Lindsay sneered. 'But you won't, will you, because you're spineless and weak. You're nothing without me.'

Sasha's gaze shifted to Chloe, her heart heavy with the weight of the situation. In Chloe's innocent eyes, she saw a reflection of the vulnerability she felt. She knew that strength was necessary – not just for her own sake, but for Chloe's future, one that deserved to be free from the hell she had endured all of her life.

'Sorry. You're right, Mum,' Sasha said, her voice

steady despite how she felt inside. 'I should've cleared it with you first. It won't happen again.'

Her mother's smirk remained, but Sasha refused to let it break her resolve. She scooped up Chloe, put her jacket on, and placed her in her buggy.

'See you later,' Sasha said, mustering a small smile before walking away.

As she stepped outside, the cool breeze brushed against her face, bringing a sense of clarity. Sasha knew she couldn't endure this toxic environment for much longer.

Her plan to escape had to be set in motion sooner than she had anticipated.

Chapter Thirteen

Hailey browsed the perfume section with excitement and uncertainty. She had never purchased perfume before, not even for herself, but she wanted to find something special for Sasha. She sampled each tester, attempting to envision which scent would best suit her.

The idea of choosing perfume as a thank-you gift for Sasha's kindness the previous night had struck Hailey while researching thoughtful gifts for women of her age. Perfume had ranked at the top of the list, and Hailey believed it would make the perfect present.

Finally, she stumbled upon a fragrance that she thought Sasha would love.

'This one smells amazing,' Hailey murmured.

With the chosen perfume cradled in her hand, Hailey proceeded to the check-out where she completed the purchase. Exiting the department store, she found a nearby café for lunch. Settling at a table, she arranged her food and drink before retrieving her phone from her pocket and dialling a familiar number.

After a couple of rings, her call was answered.

'Hello,' came the voice on the other end.

'Hi, Christine.'

'Lovely to hear from you. How is everything?'

'Great. Lindsay bought me a new phone. I just wanted to let you know I'll be getting a new number once it's all set up.'

'That's quite thoughtful of her.'

'Yeah, it is. I've arranged for flowers to be delivered to her to say thanks,' Hailey said, taking a sip of her coffee.

'I'm glad everything's going smoothly.'

'Yeah, they're an incredible family,' Hailey said, firmly putting the unexpected mishap at dinner out of her mind.

There was a brief pause before Christine continued, 'Well, it sounds like things are really falling into place.'

'Definitely.'

As their conversation flowed, Hailey was careful not to mention Sasha by name. She didn't want Christine to sense the depth of her feelings for her. It wasn't that she wanted to keep secrets, but she feared that revealing too much might complicate things. She was still trying to make sense of everything herself.

'I seem to be having a run of good luck at the moment. I found a job today as a waitress in a new restaurant that's opening next week. It's all thanks to you, you know,' Hailey said, feeling a deep sense of appreciation for Christine's role in her life.

Christine's response was both humble and sincere. 'I may have provided some support, but it's your determination and hard work that got you this job, Hailey. You should be proud of yourself. How are you getting along with Sasha?'

'Yeah, good. We're going to the cinema tomorrow.'

'That's great. Any particular movie you're looking forward to seeing?' Christine said.

'Nah, we're taking baby Chloe, so it'll be something

suitable for her.'

After a momentary silence Christine asked, 'Oh, are you both babysitting for Lindsay while she goes out?'

'No. Lindsay needs Sasha to take care of Chloe while she works on her new book.'

Christine's voice carried a hint of concern. 'Oh, right. I would've thought that being Sasha's weekend off from university, she would be enjoying some downtime.'

'To be honest, I don't think she gets much of a break. She seems to look after Chloe a lot,' Hailey said, her tone thoughtful. 'But she loves her little sister, so I'm sure she doesn't mind.'

'That's all very well, but why can't Chloe's father look after her?'

'I get the impression that no one thinks he's capable. He just wants to keep out the way for an easy life.'

'Ah, like most men do.'

Hailey laughed. 'True.'

'Well, I'm sure you'll have a nice time.'

'We will.'

As their conversation drew to a close, Christine's innocent question had triggered a sense of doubt. From what Hailey had observed so far, it appeared that Sasha carried a significant amount of responsibility when it came to taking care of Chloe.

A gnawing unease settled within her, akin to a puzzle with missing pieces she couldn't fit into place. Not yet, anyway.

Chapter Fourteen

Sasha groaned as she took in her reflection in the mirror. Every outfit she had tried on that morning, and there had been at least seven, just didn't look right. She was aiming for casual but smart, but the mismatched top and bottoms looked at odds with one another. She sighed, frustration building as she tossed another rejected outfit onto her bed.

Before she had time to change yet again, there was a tap on the door. She glanced over at the clock – two p.m. on the dot.

'This will have to do,' she said with a resigned smile, giving herself a final once-over before opening the door.

'Hey, Sasha!' Hailey said, her eyes quickly scanning Sasha before meeting her gaze.

Sasha felt a pang of self-consciousness, wondering if Hailey had noticed her struggle to put an outfit together.

'Hey,' she replied.

'You look great.'

Sasha tried to suppress her surprise at the compliment. She looked down at her outfit and then back at Hailey. 'Oh, um, thanks. I couldn't really decide on what to wear.'

Hailey laughed. 'I know the feeling. Sometimes it's like my wardrobe is conspiring against me.'

Sasha smiled, feeling a little more at ease. 'Exactly.

It's like all the clothes I usually love just decided to rebel today.'

'Are you ready to go, or are you going to change again?' Hailey said, eyeing the pile of clothes on her bed.

'No, I'm done. Let me just get Chloe, and I'll meet you outside.'

'Okie dokie.'

Together, they descended the stairs, only to split up and head in opposite directions upon reaching the bottom. Sasha felt a wave of relief as she spotted Chloe with her dad, her mother conspicuously absent.

'We're gonna be off now,' Sasha said, collecting Chloe from her dad's arms.

'Have a nice day.'

'We will.' How couldn't she? There was no way she could ignore the excitement bubbling within her. After all, she was about to spend a few hours of quality time with Hailey. The thought alone brought a smile to her face.

As they eased into the car, the radio played a Taylor Swift ballad that resonated with Sasha's emotions, its gentle melody tugging at her heartstrings. Little did Hailey know, every note seemed to intensify Sasha's growing attraction to her.

They drove along in comfortable silence until Sasha noticed the different route they were taking.

'You're going the wrong way. You should have turned off; the cinema is down there.'

A playful glint appeared in Hailey's eyes as she met Sasha's gaze. 'We aren't going to the cinema.'

'So, where are we headed?'

'For a picnic.'

Sasha's eyes widened. 'A picnic?'

'Yep, it's too nice to be indoors.'

'You're right about that.'

The drive continued, and Sasha stole glances at Hailey, admiring her confident driving skills and how well she navigated the road. She couldn't help but notice how Hailey's tight-fitted crop top showcased her toned physique either. Sasha felt a subtle heat rise to her cheeks. She was paying a bit more attention to Hailey than she'd intended, so she stared straight ahead for the rest of the journey.

Once they arrived at a scenic spot that overlooked a tranquil lake bordered by lush greenery, Hailey pulled the car to a stop. She stepped out and walked to the rear of the car as Sasha headed to fetch Chloe. Minutes later, Hailey laid down a chequered throw and opened the hamper she'd brought.

'Voilà! Our little lakeside feast,' Hailey said with a grin as she laid out an assortment of sandwiches, snacks, and drinks within easy reach.

'You really have thought of everything, haven't you?' Sasha said.

'Picnics are my speciality,' Hailey replied with a wink as she popped a grape into her mouth.

'This place is amazing,' Sasha said, her gaze sweeping over the serene landscape.

Hailey smiled. 'I come here whenever I need a break from the city chaos. It's like a little slice of paradise.'

'I can see why,' Sasha said, stroking Chloe's cheek and smiling down at her.

'You'll make a great mum someday.'

'You think so?'

'Absolutely. The way you care for Chloe is off the scales.'

'Chloe is Chloe. Having my own …' Sasha gave a small shake of her head, '… not so sure.'

'Yeah, true,' Hailey said, a grin on her face. 'So, what do you do for fun?'

'Oh, um, nothing much.'

Hailey's brow furrowed in a playful challenge. 'Come on, you must do something. What about dating?'

Sasha nervously pulled at a loose thread on her jeans. She wasn't sure if she was ready to dive into this topic, but there was something about the easy camaraderie between her and Hailey that made her want to open up.

'Urgh, dating. It's not exactly my area of expertise,' Sasha admitted, forcing a small laugh.

'If you don't want to talk about it …'

'No, I do,' Sasha said quickly, surprising herself with her honesty. 'It's just that … I've never really been on a proper date before.'

Hailey's eyes widened in surprise, but her expression remained kind and supportive. 'You're kidding?'

Sasha shook her head. 'No one's ever asked me.'

'Have *you* asked anyone?'

Sasha felt a twinge of embarrassment. 'Well, no. But I do kinda have a crush on my personal tutor.'

'Oh, right. What's his name?'

Hailey's casual question hung in the air, and Sasha's stomach dropped at the realization that Hailey assumed her crush was on a guy. The moment suddenly felt like a crossroads, a choice that Sasha had to make.

She looked at Hailey, her mind racing.

Shall I tell her?

She had shared so much already, but this felt like an entirely different territory. Revealing her sexuality was always going to be a significant moment. Up until now, Sasha had only told her Aunt Jo, who she knew would be supportive and understanding about it.

'Sasha?'

The fear of rejection and judgment clenched at her heart, but still, something inside her urged her to be honest.

Sasha took a deep breath, her gaze fixed on her hands. 'Actually, it's not a "his". It's a "her". Her name is Dr Anderson.'

Sasha held her breath, waiting for Hailey's reaction.

'Oh, right. Sorry!'

Sasha glanced up, relief flooding through her as she met Hailey's warm gaze. It wasn't judgment she saw there, but rather genuine acceptance.

'I should really know better.'

Sasha's curiosity piqued. 'What do you mean?'

'I'm into girls too,' Hailey said with a confident smile.

Sasha's heart skipped a beat.

'You are?'

Hailey nodded, her smile widening. 'Why d'you look so shocked?'

'I don't know… I just…'

Hailey laughed and nudged Sasha's shoulder. 'It's okay.'

Their eyes met, and in that shared moment, Sasha felt a connection that transcended words.

'Thanks for sharing that with me,' Hailey said, her voice soft and sincere.

'I'm glad I did.'

A feeling a warmth spread throughout Sasha's body.

'So,' Sasha began, a mischievous grin forming on her lips, 'are you dating anyone?'

'No, not at the moment. I've never had a proper relationship either.'

Sasha laughed. 'We are both as hopeless as each other.'

'You can say that again.'

Sasha shook her head with a smile. As they continued to chat, she realised that this was more than just a picnic – it was a turning point in her life, a moment that had the potential to change everything.

Chapter Fifteen

'You seem happy,' Jo observed, her eyes meeting Sasha's.

The corners of Sasha's lips turned upward, the joy she felt too infectious to contain.

'That's because I am.'

Jo extended a rinsed plate towards Sasha, who promptly accepted it, dried it, and placed it in its designated spot among the neatly arranged kitchenware.

'It must be nice having someone your own age staying in the house.'

'It is. Hailey is amazing.'

'More amazing than Dr Anderson?' Jo teased playfully.

Sasha laughed. 'Oh, much more. That was just a silly crush.'

A knowing glint danced in Jo's eyes as she leaned in slightly. 'And am I sensing that you might have something more than just friendship feelings for Hailey?'

Sasha's cheeks flushed. 'Well, I … I'm not sure. It's all quite new and … complicated.'

'Ah, the complexities of the heart. It's a journey we all must navigate.'

'Yeah, exactly. It's just … I never expected to feel this way.'

Jo spoke as she put away the cutlery. 'Feelings have a way of surprising us. Just remember that the heart often knows what the mind is still trying to comprehend.'

Sasha hesitated for a moment, then shrugged. 'Maybe.'

Jo's hand found its way to Sasha's shoulder, a gesture of comfort and support. 'You deserve to find happiness, Sasha. It's really unfair how Lindsay treats you.'

Sasha's shoulders sagged slightly. 'It won't be like this forever. You know I can't leave Chloe.'

'I wish there was more I could do to help you.'

'Just having your support is enough.' A wistful sigh escaped Sasha's lips as she mused, 'Sometimes, I can't help but wish I had an older brother or sister to share the load with me.'

An uncomfortable expression flitted across Jo's features, her gaze momentarily flickering away from Sasha's before she turned her back, occupying herself with the task of wiping down the worktop.

I shouldn't have said that. Jo doesn't exactly have the best relationship with my dad.

'It's getting late,' Jo said, nodding toward a bin liner full of clothes in the corner. 'You sure you can manage?'

Sasha playfully flexed her muscles. 'I don't work out for nothing, you know.'

Jo laughed. 'You'll be entering bodybuilding competitions soon.'

With a grin, Sasha slipped on her coat and hoisted the bag over her shoulder.

They walked to the front door side by side.

'Keep me updated about how things are with Hailey,' Jo said.

'I will.'

They held each other in a tight embrace before Sasha set off home, deciding to take the shortcut through the alleyway, a route she had taken countless times in the past without a second thought. But tonight, an inexplicable unease hung in the air, causing her to quicken her pace as she started down the dimly lit path.

The flickering glow of street lamps cast elongated and unsettling shadows, seemingly trailing her every move. A shiver travelled down her spine, the sense of someone watching her intensifying with each step she took. She glanced over her shoulder and saw what she thought was someone walking behind her.

Sasha took out her phone, her fingers shaking as she called her dad.

'Come on, Dad. Pick up,' she whispered urgently to herself.

She looked around, her eyes darting between the shadows that seemed to dance with an eerie rhythm. Every footfall felt amplified in the silence, echoing like a sinister whisper.

After several rings, the call went to voicemail.

'Shit!'

Maybe Hailey will help.

Desperation taking hold, Sasha swiftly dialled Hailey's number.

'Please pick up, Hailey.'

Finally, on the third ring, Hailey's voice came through. 'Hey, Sasha. What's up?'

'Hailey,' Sasha said, trying to keep her voice steady, 'I think someone's following me. I'm scared.'

'What? Are you serious?' Hailey's tone shifted, all traces of casualness gone.

'Yeah, I'm sure of it,' Sasha replied, glancing over her shoulder anxiously. 'I don't know what to do.'

'Okay, stay calm,' Hailey said, her voice now firm and reassuring. 'Tell me exactly where you are, and I'll come and get you.'

'I'm walking down the alley that leads onto Pine Street. There's a coffee shop called Beano's on the corner.'

'I know it. Listen, I'm on my way.' Hailey's voice carried a sense of urgency. 'Just keep moving, and don't look back. I'll be there as fast as I can.'

Relief flooded her. 'Thank you, Hailey. Please hurry.'

Without thinking, Sasha broke into a run, desperate to escape the oppressive atmosphere of the alleyway.

Sasha emerged onto the safety of the well-lit main street and paused for a moment, taking in deep breaths in an attempt to steady her racing heart and quiet the tumultuous thoughts swirling in her mind.

Crossing the street, she approached the bus stop where a small cluster of people had gathered, waiting for the next bus. Yet, despite the presence of others, Sasha couldn't shake the lingering sense of vulnerability that had taken hold of her. Each passing minute felt like hours, and her anxiety steadily rose as she scanned her surroundings.

And then, like a beacon of hope, the familiar sight of Hailey's car appeared in the distance, cutting through the darkness of the night.

Hailey pulled up beside the bus stop, and Sasha quickly jumped in, her breath catching in her throat. 'Drive, please, just drive.'

Hailey didn't waste a second and slammed her foot on the accelerator.

'Are you okay?' Hailey asked, briefly looking at Sasha.

'I don't know,' Sasha said, her voice shaking. 'That's the first time something like this has ever happened to me before. It was so creepy.'

The once familiar streets now seemed menacing. Sasha's heart pounded even harder as she glanced out the car window. The dim streetlights illuminated a mysterious figure in a dark hoodie, just as she had feared.

'Hailey, look!' Sasha shouted, pointing out the window. 'That's him, the guy in the hoodie. Should we call the police?'

'No point. He'll probably be gone by the time they show up, that's if they'd even come. You're safe now, just try and relax,' Hailey said firmly.

Sasha closed her eyes and inhaled deeply. The last thing she felt at that moment in time was anything but safe.

As they neared home, Hailey suddenly pulled

over at the top of the street.

'Why're you pulling over? I've got to get home. I need to put Chloe to bed.'

Turning to Sasha, Hailey met her gaze directly. 'I'm sure your mum can handle it.'

'Please, Hailey, take me home.'

There was a moment of hesitation in Hailey's response. 'Sasha, tell me if I'm overstepping, but is everything okay between you and your mum?'

Sasha's guard flew up immediately. 'Yes, it's fine. Why'd you ask?'

'Just wondering,' Hailey said. 'It's just that … I've noticed you seem tense around her sometimes.'

A sigh escaped Sasha's lips, torn between opening up and holding her feelings close.

'We just have a complicated relationship,' she said. 'But really, I should get back.'

'Okay, but first …' Hailey leant over and reached into the glove compartment, producing a beautifully wrapped gift box.

'What's this?' Sasha said as she unwrapped the present, revealing the delicate bottle of perfume within. A gasp escaped her lips. 'Oh, my god, Hailey. What the … I don't know what to say. Thank you! Oh my god, I can't believe this.'

'I've been waiting for the right moment to give it to you …'

A charged atmosphere hung between them, and before Sasha could process what she was doing, she leaned in intending to plant a grateful kiss on Hailey's cheek. What happened next caught them both off guard; their lips met in a tender, unexpected kiss.

Time seemed to slow down as they pulled back, eyes locked in mutual surprise and uncertainty. Sasha's cheeks flushed, embarrassment colouring her voice.

'I'm so sorry. I didn't mean to … I mean, I just wanted to thank you for the perfume.'

Hailey gently touched Sasha's cheek. 'No need to apologise. I didn't mind at all.'

Sasha's phone pinged, interrupting the moment. She glanced down at the screen and let out an exasperated breath.

'It's my mum. She wants to know how long I'm going to be.'

Hailey nodded. Without another word, she started the car and drove them home.

The journey, though brief, felt like an eternity. Sasha couldn't shake the memory of Hailey's lips on hers, the surprising touch that had ignited something within her. She replayed the moment, trying to grasp the electrifying sensations that had surged through her.

Sasha's house soon came into view and Hailey parked the car.

Sasha didn't get out straight away. Her mind was lost in the aftermath of their kiss, trying to decipher the unspoken exchange that had left its mark on her heart.

Chapter Sixteen

In the dimly lit room, Jo remained seated in the aftermath of Sasha's departure. The street lamp's soft glow filtered through the curtains, casting a melancholic light over her cluttered living space.

Sighing, her thoughts tangled in the mysteries that haunted her for years. Sasha, her cherished niece, illuminated her life, yet Jo was laden with an unshareable truth – a truth intertwined with both Sasha's and her own past.

Her mind traced her family's complex history. Raised with Josh, her younger brother, in a turbulent and abusive household, their mother's demons inflicted lasting scars. Jo always tried to protect Josh, taking her role as a sister seriously. But his choices led him down a destructive path mirroring their mother's.

Determined to shield Sasha from their painful history, Jo had grown close to her. Their eyes reflected shared struggles, yet guilt gnawed at Jo for harbouring secrets.

Time ticked on, and Jo couldn't conceal the truth indefinitely. Unsure of how to proceed, she knew she must rescue Sasha – even if that meant confronting the dark secrets that loomed.

In the quiet room, her thoughts travelled back to the day their family fell apart. Sasha's life had been impacted since, yet Jo hesitated to expose the truth.

Until now.

Chapter Seventeen

'Must you always resort to exaggeration?' Lindsay's patience wore thin as she voiced her irritation.

Josh, in the midst of slipping on his shoes, locked eyes with her. 'I'm simply suggesting that parading Chloe around like an exhibit isn't right.'

Studying Josh's reflection in the mirror, Lindsay's expression remained unwavering. 'Josh, I need to demonstrate that I'm a successful woman who has achieved it all. Bringing Chloe along tonight is the most effective way to maintain that image.'

With a hint of sarcasm, Josh said, 'Ah, the usual sermon. Perhaps you should dress as a preacher to match the role you're playing.'

Josh's unexpected tone caught Lindsay off guard. She turned, her eyes narrow. 'Excuse me?'

Quickly retracting his words, Josh stammered, 'I … I meant that as a compliment. You know, you have an uncanny ability to provide insightful advice to people.'

'You know something, your behaviour has been rather out of character since Hailey arrived. Is there something you'd like to tell me?'

Defensively, Josh retorted, 'Like what?'

'Don't play with me. I've noticed how you look at her. Are you trying to recapture your youth or something?' Lindsay snorted. 'As if she'd even look at someone like you.'

For a prolonged moment, Josh stared at Lindsay in astonishment.

Then, he let out an incredulous breath.

'You truly are warped. Do you know that? Hailey's the same age as Sasha. How could you even think that I could … I can't even finish the sentence; it's utterly repugnant.'

Lindsay's expression remained unimpressed and unconvinced. 'If you say so. Let's go.'

Descending the stairs, Lindsay found Sasha and Hailey loitering in the hallway.

'Don't you think it's a bit late to be taking Chloe out?' Sasha said.

Lindsay offered her a reassuring smile.

'Chloe will be well taken care of. Why don't you girls have a fun night in and watch some TV?'

'But Mum—'

Lindsay's tone turned saccharine. 'It's time you two enjoyed yourselves. Josh, grab Chloe. I don't want to be late. My fans are waiting.'

The bookstore was filled with excitement as Lindsay and Josh made their entrance. The room exuded a cosy charm, its warm-toned walls lined with bookshelves boasting an array of literature. Rows of chairs were neatly arranged, facing a podium at the front, where Lindsay would soon take centre stage.

Lindsay's fans, spanning various ages and backgrounds, were already present, conversing animatedly. Some clutched well-worn copies of her past works, eager for an autograph. Admiration permeated the air, as if

Lindsay's very presence had the power to transform the evening into an unforgettable experience.

As Lindsay stepped in front of the crowd, a ripple of applause cascaded through the audience. She exuded elegance in her attire, her confidence palpable with each step. Graciously acknowledging the applause, she settled behind the podium, prompting the crowd to hush in anticipation.

Expressing gratitude for the attendees, Lindsay's words elicited smiles and nods. As she recounted her writing journey, her fans hung on to every word, captivated by her storytelling prowess.

Her speech gained momentum, building towards an eagerly awaited moment.

Lindsay skilfully paused, allowing her words to resonate before revealing her surprise. 'Tonight, I have a special announcement to share. As some of you may know, my writing has always mirrored my experiences – my triumphs and tribulations.'

The room held its breath, curiosity rippling through the air. Lindsay's gaze swept over her audience. 'I've made a decision to embark on a new journey: a journey to write my own biography.'

Surprise gasps were succeeded by enthusiastic applause.

Lindsay's voice wove vulnerability and strength as she continued.

'My biography will delve into the depths of my upbringing, my struggles, and my triumphs over adversity. I aim to share my story – the tale of a woman who transcended a challenging past within the foster care system to become the person I am today.'

Chapter Eighteen

The living room was dimly lit, the glow from the TV casting a warm ambience across their faces. Hailey and Sasha sat side by side on the sofa, their backs nestled in the comfort of the cushions. What should have been a relaxed and carefree evening, a chance for them to unwind and forget about the world outside, was marred by unspoken tension. Ever since their surprising first kiss, an undercurrent of awkwardness had seeped into what used to be an effortless friendship.

Hailey stared at the movie playing on the screen, trying to focus on the plot, on anything other than the growing unease between them. When an intimate scene unfolded, Hailey's gaze briefly shifted from the characters to Sasha, who seemed equally captivated. Heat rising to her cheeks, Hailey swallowed hard, suddenly acutely aware of every inch of space between them.

This was the chance to break the silence and confront the unspoken.

Hailey shifted slightly on the sofa, her eyes still fixed on the television. After a moment's pause, she let out a small laugh, her voice breaking the stillness like a pebble skipping across a pond.

'Kissing's funny, isn't it?' Hailey mused.

Sasha turned to look at her. 'Funny? In what way?'

'Think about it. We pucker up our lips, tilt our heads, and basically press our faces together. It's like a secret handshake, but for the lips.'

Sasha's laughter bubbled up, the tension that had gripped the room slowly giving way to genuine amusement.

'You're right! And there's this whole unwritten manual of rules, like, do you go left or right? Is there an optimal angle? How long? Tongue or no tongue? It's like a dance routine without any rehearsals.'

'Exactly!' Hailey said, her laughter joining Sasha's. 'Not to mention the awkward nose bump or teeth clink that happens from time to time.'

They both dissolved into giggles.

'And don't even get me started on the pressure to make it all romantic and magical,' Sasha added, wiping away a tear of laughter. 'Like, if you believe movies, every kiss should have fireworks in the background or a chorus of singing birds.'

Summoning every ounce of courage, Hailey cleared her throat, her voice coming out softer than she intended. 'Well, I have to admit … I kind of experienced that when we kissed.'

A nervous laugh escaped Sasha's lips. 'Really?'

'Didn't you feel it too?'

'Yeah.'

The admission hung in the air.

'I don't want things to be weird between us, Sasha. You're a great friend and I don't want anything to ruin it.'

Sasha's eyes held a warmth that melted away some of Hailey's anxiety.

'I feel the same way. You mean a lot to me, and I don't want anything to change that either.'

'So, where does that leave us? With the kiss, I mean.'

'I don't know about you, but …' Sasha closed the gap between them. 'It leaves me wanting to kiss you again.'

A moment of profound stillness enveloped them. Hailey's heart raced, a mixture of emotions swirling within her chest – surprise, longing, and the undeniable pull of attraction.

For a beat, the world seemed to shrink, the dimly lit living room becoming their entire universe. Without hesitation, Hailey leaned in, her eyes locked onto Sasha's lips. The tension that had once lingered between them dissipated, and their lips met in a tender kiss.

'Maybe kissing isn't so funny after all,' Hailey said.

Hailey's breath caught as Sasha's hand guided hers to rest softly against Sasha's left breast. 'Can you feel my heart beating?'

Closing her eyes for a brief moment, Hailey focused on the sensation beneath her hand. 'I can.'

Sasha's gaze dropped to Hailey's mouth, then shifted back to her eyes, only to return once more to her lips. 'I want you.'

Before she could react, Sasha unbuttoned her shirt, exposing her smooth cleavage, her erect nipples straining against the lace material of her bra. Her hand combed through Hailey's hair as she crushed her lips against Hailey's again with an intensity that took her by surprise. Sasha's full weight pushed Hailey down back against the sofa, mounting her as the kiss deepened.

'Touch me,' she breathed into Hailey's mouth, arching impatiently against Hailey's hand.

Slowly, Hailey slid her hand into Sasha's underwear, her finger gently caressing Sasha's wet folds.

Sasha buried her face in the crook of Hailey's neck, her skin hot and clammy.

'Oh, yeah.'

Hailey parted her with two fingers and found her clit, rubbing it in small circles as Sasha's ragged breath sounded in her ear. Riding her hand, Sasha pushed down harder and Hailey's fingers easily slid inside her as she thrust back and forth in a steady rhythm.

Hailey could feel her own hot fluid between her legs as she squeezed herself against the muscle of Sasha's thigh.

In a frenzy of passion, Sasha lifted up Hailey's T-shirt, revealing her braless, pert breasts. She took one of Hailey's nipples in her mouth, causing Hailey to gasp loudly. Spurred on by Hailey's reaction, Sasha slid down the sofa and tugged down Hailey's jeans and underwear, revealing her glistening labia.

Sasha glanced up at Hailey, a brief flicker of uncertainty clouding her eyes.

'I've never done this before.'

Hailey offered a comforting smile.

'Don't worry, neither have I.'

Sasha smiled, then lowered her mouth between Hailey's legs.

As the tip of Sasha's tongue hit Hailey's clit, a ripple of ecstasy shot through her.

Oh my god!

With every flick, Hailey edged closer and closer to climax. All the painful memories and shadows from her past dissolved into insignificance, consumed by the intensity of Sasha's touch and the depth of intimacy they shared.

When Sasha's fingers plunged inside her, Hailey finally let go, her body and mind colliding in a symphony of raw emotion and unbridled vulnerability. Hailey's muscles contracted around Sasha's fingers, holding on to every last ounce of pleasure.

Sasha moved back up beside Hailey, both out of breath and still desperate for more. Hailey pulled Sasha in for a kiss, the taste of her own juices still lingering on Sasha's lips. She slid her hand back inside Sasha's underwear and was surprised at how wet she was.

Sasha smiled in acknowledgement. 'That's what you do to me.'

They continued to kiss, their tongues dancing in a sensuous rhythm as Hailey furiously rubbed and caressed Sasha's swollen nub until, with an unbridled cry, Sasha bucked and writhed against Hailey's touch.

Lying side by side, their faces adorned with contented smiles, they exchanged glances.

'I can't believe I waited so long for this to happen,'

Hailey said.

'Was it worth the wait?'

Hailey leaned closer, planting a sensual kiss on Sasha's lips.

'Definitely. I can't believe it was your first time. You really know how to use your tongue.'

Sasha laughed. 'I wouldn't mind some more practice.'

'Anytime. I'm happy to be your guinea pig.'

Sasha's grin widened. 'I'm also willing to be a guinea pig, whenever you feel ready.'

Hailey's hand slid up to cup Sasha's breast. Her lips grazing Sasha's as she spoke.

'I'm ready now.'

Sasha placed her warm, moist lips against Hailey's once more, her tongue slipping inside Hailey's mouth. An urgent, pulsating sensation arose between Hailey's thighs at the thought of tasting Sasha.

Suddenly, Sasha pulled away.

'Shit. We'd better not. They're gonna be home soon. Have you seen the time?'

'God, no. That would've been a bit embarrassing if they walked in on us.'

'More than just embarrassing.'

Hailey chose not to delve deeper into what Sasha implied. That conversation could wait for another moment.

Adjusting her position slightly, Sasha propped herself up on her elbow. 'So, what happens now?'

Hailey shrugged. 'I have no idea. I guess we just

continue with our lives as normal.'

'But what's "normal" for us?'

Hailey laughed. 'Honestly, I don't really know. I'm the last person who would know what a healthy relationship should look like.'

Sasha's gaze held a hint of fragility as she ventured further. 'So, are you my girlfriend now?'

'Is that what you want?'

Sasha's response was swift and sure. 'Absolutely.'

'Then it's settled. We're officially girlfriends.'

A giggle escaped Sasha's lips. 'I really like the sound of that.'

'Me too,' Hailey agreed as she pulled Sasha to her.

Chapter Nineteen

Diary entry:

Remember that night with Sasha? Yeah, still can't get it out of my head. It's like every touch, every moment, is etched into my brain.

But guess what? Between work and uni, we NEVER see each other alone. Those stolen glances and secret smiles are all we've got at the moment and it's killing me inside. I've thought about sneaking into her room at night, but I've been too scared of getting caught. The last thing I need at the moment is to get thrown out of the house.

And don't even get me started on Lindsay. She's ALWAYS around, nose deep in her new book, making it impossible for me and Sasha to find a moment alone.

Honestly, it's so frustrating. For the first time in my life, I've met someone who gets me, but we just can't be together. Not yet anyway. But you know what? I'm not giving up. That night meant something, and I'm not letting it go that easily.

Thinking back, it took some serious guts to let Sasha in like that. I mean, I've got so much locked up inside and

I finally feel able to talk to someone about it and not be judged. It's, like, thrilling and terrifying all at once. But I guess that's what makes it worth it, right?

As I'm scribbling this down, I can't help but wonder what's next for us. Are we gonna figure out how to make this work, or is life gonna keep messing with us? Either way, I'm grateful for the moments we've had, for the way Sasha's turned my world upside down.

Who knows? Maybe one day these pages won't just be full of my rants. Maybe they'll tell the story of us, the obstacles we faced, and how we came out on the other side. Fingers crossed!

Chapter Twenty

The following days flowed by uneventfully. Lindsay was at home constantly, writing her new book, and Sasha had hardly seen Hailey, who worked evenings. Sasha was counting down the minutes until she could spend quality time with Hailey again. Their first time together had been like an addictive rush, a feeling she couldn't shake off. She'd thought it would be awkward and embarrassing, but it had been nothing like that. It was like a surge of electricity, a connection she'd never felt before. And that's why she'd made up her mind. They needed to escape the confines of the house, to find a space where it was just the two of them.

Sasha entered the kitchen and spotted Lindsay by the worktop, preparing tea, while Josh was sliding into his jacket. 'You going out, Dad?'

'Yeah, the transmission fluid is leaking again,' Josh said, shaking his head. 'I'm going to pop into the garage quickly and see what's wrong.'

'You know I'm going out,' Sasha said once Josh had left. 'So, I won't be able to put Chloe down for the night. I put it in your calendar.'

She thought to remind her mother just in case Lindsay decided to use it against her again, implying that she didn't give her enough notice beforehand.

Sasha accidentally dipped her finger in a small puddle of water on the worktop and wiped her fingers on the tea towel.

'What did you just do?' Lindsay asked, her eyelids batting rapidly.

'What? I wiped my hands.'

'On the tea towel. Are you stupid? It's for drying dishes. How clean would the dishes be if I dried them with a dirty cloth? Being stupid is not exactly an excuse for lacking common sense, is it?'

Oh, here we go again.

Instead of answering, Sasha swallowed hard and bit her lip.

'Sasha, quick! I need your help!' Hailey said, hurrying into the kitchen.

'What's wrong?'

'My zip is caught. Help me, please,' Hailey said, turning to expose her bare back.

'Hailey! I was talking to Sasha! I'd appreciate it if you didn't interrupt us in the future!'

'Oh, sorry, I didn't realise.'

The doorbell rang.

'I suppose I should answer the door too, shall I?'

'It's all right. It's our taxi,' Sasha said.

'Taxi?' Lindsay said.

'Yeah, we're going into town for a quiz night. We'll be back by midnight,' Sasha said, her words carrying a touch of excitement.

Without awaiting a response, Sasha swiftly zipped up Hailey's top and guided her towards the front door.

'Your mum didn't look happy in the slightest.

I'd hate to see her face if she found out you lied to her,' Hailey said once they were comfortably settled inside the taxi.

'Who cares. Now, can we put my mother aside for a moment and focus on us?'

'Sure, fine by me.'

Leaning in closer, Sasha whispered into Hailey's ear, her voice laden with anticipation, 'So, when we get to the hotel, the first thing I want to do is take a bubble bath with you.'

Hailey laughed and responded in a whisper, 'Why a bubble bath?'

'Because I've always thought it looked so romantic in films.'

Hailey tilted her head playfully. 'Do you happen to have a bottle of bubbles in that bag of yours?'

Sasha's bag revealed an assortment of goodies, eliciting Hailey's surprise. 'Wow, you've really come prepared, haven't you?'

Sasha nodded with a grin, closing her bag resolutely. 'We've got six hours to enjoy our time together. I want to make the most of every moment.'

Fifteen minutes later, they entered their hotel room, Sasha wasting no time in dashing to the king-sized bed and executing a playful belly flop.

'Oh my god, I feel so free!' Sasha exclaimed with glee.

Hailey joined her on the bed, her hand sliding up Sasha's skirt as a mischievous twinkle danced in her eyes. 'Do you mind if we skip the bath?'

A faux expression of disappointment crossed Sasha's features. 'Oh, what did you have in mind instead?'

'Come closer and I'll show you,' Hailey whispered, pulling her in until their lips met, covering Sasha's mouth with her own in a fervent kiss. Her tongue probed Sasha's mouth, as her hand ran through her hair.

'I've not stopped thinking about tasting you,' Hailey said. 'Every night, I've just laid in bed wondering if I should creep into your room.'

'I wish you had.'

'I didn't want to risk getting caught.'

'That's all part of the fun.'

'Don't worry. I made the most of the fantasy.'

Sasha leaned back, a salacious smile crossing her features.

'Show me what you did.'

'What!? No!'

Hailey's cheeks flushed crimson.

Sasha gently stroked Hailey's face.

'It would really turn me on.'

Hailey hesitated; then, slowly, her hand glided downward between her thighs, her eyes staying locked onto Sasha's. Sasha watched as Hailey hitched up her skirt and eased down her underwear. She began touching herself, slowly at first, then more forcefully. The intensity grew between Sasha's thighs as she watched, prompting her to remove her own clothes.

She lay there naked, taking in the beautiful woman beside her. The room seemed to hold its breath as she let her gaze wander over Hailey's form – the gentle curves, the soft lines, the imperfections that made her uniquely perfect. Sasha reached out, her fingers grazing Hailey's skin with a tender touch.

As Hailey's breathing became more rapid, signalling the inevitable, Sasha decided to slow the pace.

'Don't come yet,' Sasha whispered. 'Why don't we make your fantasy a reality?'

Desire burned in Hailey's eyes and she motioned for Sasha to straddle her.

Sasha positioned herself over Hailey's mouth, maintaining a tantalizing distance that left Hailey unable to make contact.

'You are just teasing me now,' Hailey whined.

Sasha smirked, then lowered herself, a wave of euphoria hitting her as her clit made contact with Hailey's warm tongue.

Hailey devoured Sasha, licking and sucking, then darting deep inside her. Sasha's body felt alive in a way she never thought possible.

Everything washed away in that moment. Her mother, her father, Chloe, university ... She was reaching heights she could never even imagine.

Sasha gripped the headboard tightly as she rode Hailey's tongue, eventually succumbing to the feeling and climaxing hard against Hailey's mouth. At the same time, Hailey cried out in pleasure, her body shaking under Sasha's weight.

'Hey, I thought I said not to come yet!'

Sasha tumbled to the side next to Hailey.

Hailey's breath came in heavy gasps, her face flushed a vivid red from the exertion.

'Sorry, I couldn't help myself. That was so much better than the fantasy.'

Naked and entwined, Sasha nestled herself against Hailey's body in a tender embrace.

'I want to lie here with you like this forever.'

'Even when I'm old and toothless?'

'Even then,' Sasha said with conviction.

'You're a "forever" kind of girl, aren't you?'

Sasha's insecurity crept in. 'Does that bother you?'

'Nope. You're used to it, so you don't understand how reassuring it feels.'

A sigh escaped Sasha's lips, and she shifted onto her back, staring up at the ceiling. Hailey's concern was immediate. 'Hey, what's wrong?'

'Nothing,' Sasha replied, her voice soft but with the weight of something deeper evident in her tone.

'Don't hide from me, Sasha,' Hailey said. 'D'you think I tend to wallow in self-pity too much?'

Startled by the question, Sasha turned her gaze to Hailey.

'What? No, of course not,' she said quickly, her hand reaching out to tenderly tuck a strand of hair behind Hailey's ear. 'It's not about that. It's just that you seem to think I have this perfect life with a perfect family, and that couldn't be further from the truth.'

'I know your mum can be intense and tactless—'

'It's more than that.' Sasha sighed again. 'I don't know how to explain it.'

'Try.'

'Okay, I think … I think my mum hates me.'

There. She'd said it out loud for the first time in her life, and she meant every word.

Hailey burst out laughing. 'You're kidding, right?'

'No, I'm not.'

'Sasha, if your mum hated you, you'd have been raised in a place like where I grew up. The fact that you're eighteen and haven't been thrown out to fend for yourself speaks volumes.'

I knew she wouldn't understand. I wish I hadn't said anything.

'Let's forget about it.'

A sudden thought crossed Sasha's mind: What if Hailey unintentionally let slip her feelings to her mum one day, not out of malice, but with the genuine belief that it could help? Such a revelation, however well-intentioned, could potentially amplify the already complex situation by tenfold, if that was even possible.

Hailey's voice broke through Sasha's thoughts, soothing and understanding. 'No, if you want to talk about it, I'm listening. I shouldn't have said anything. Your feelings are valid …'

Sasha's voice wavered. 'Even if you think they're wrong?'

'Even then.'

Anxiousness nipped at Sasha, prompting her to check the time, her actions serving as a distraction. 'Look at the time. We've only got a few hours left.'

'It's your fault for being so good in bed.'

Laughter danced between them. 'Flattery will get you everywhere.'

Hailey climbed off the bed and extended her hand. 'Let's go …?'

'Where?'

'To have that bubble bath.'

'Oh, I thought we could—'

'We can, in the bath.' Hailey's gaze held a suggestive glint.

'In that case, you run it. I need to get my energy back.'

'Don't take too long,' Hailey teased.

She watched as Hailey moved gracefully, her nude form disappearing into the bathroom, the sound of running water following suit.

Sasha's mind was suddenly tinged with guilt, but the sound of Hailey's singing swept away her reservations. It was a moment of self-focus, a realisation that she deserved her own happiness, even in the midst of her plans involving Chloe. She wasn't forgetting her; she was just reclaiming a piece of herself. She was allowed to enjoy life.

And that's exactly what she intended to do.

Hailey appeared at the door, beckoning Sasha towards her with a seductive smile.

Starting right now.

Chapter Twenty-One

D iary entry:

I can't believe it's possible to feel this happy. Every moment with Sasha is like a dream I never want to wake up from. It's like my heart is constantly doing a happy dance, and I find myself smiling for no reason at all. With her, everything just clicks into place and …

A gentle tap on the door disrupted Hailey's writing flow. Swiftly, she shut her diary, carefully sliding it beneath her pillow. 'Come in.'

Lindsay entered, a friendly smile on her face.

'Hey, Hailey,' Lindsay said, stepping into the room. 'I was thinking, how about you join me for lunch today?'

Hailey blinked in surprise. She wondered what had prompted this sudden invitation. 'Lunch? Sure, that sounds great. Is everything okay?'

'Of course, everything's fine. I just thought it would be nice to catch up. It feels like I've barely seen you since you started working.'

'Yeah, things have been pretty hectic,' Hailey said.

'Great, I'll book a table. One, okay?'

'Sounds perfect.'

Lindsay gave a nod and backed out the room.

Hailey couldn't help but feel a tinge of disappointment that Sasha was at university today, as it would have been nice for the three of them to enjoy the day together. Hailey slipped out of bed and headed to the bathroom for a quick shower.

At one o'clock, they were ushered to a table in the high-end restaurant Lindsay had reserved. As Hailey settled into her seat, she couldn't help but be in awe of her surroundings. This place was seriously impressive! When Lindsay had mentioned lunch, Hailey had imagined something more on the cheap and cheerful side, like a burger restaurant. The reality was far beyond her expectations. She'd only ever seen places like this on TV shows or glossy magazines. She had never pictured herself actually dining in such a place. Ever.

'So, how's work?' Lindsay said, her attention divided between the menu and Hailey.

'Work's going great. I've never spent so much time on my feet before, but I'm not complaining. I feel lucky to have a job.'

Lindsay laughed. 'I remember being a broke student, waitressing twelve-hour days. Now it's all about battling backaches from sitting at my desk for hours.'

The waiter arrived, gracefully presented a bottle of wine, and poured two glasses before taking their orders. Hailey chose dishes whose names she could confidently pronounce, while Lindsay chose an exotic option that Hailey had never even come across before.

'Cheers,' Lindsay said, lifting her glass in a toast.

'Cheers,' Hailey echoed, bringing her glass to her lips and taking a cautious sip. In truth, she would have preferred a soft drink, as alcohol didn't quite agree with her. It didn't take much more than a single glass to push her over the edge.

'I just wanted to say how much I enjoyed our conversation the other night. I'm so pleased that you felt you could open up to me.'

'It was nice to know that you cared.'

'I do very much.' Lindsay leaned forward slightly. 'One thing I never got to ask was where your foster father was in all of this? I mean, was he okay with you being taken into care?'

Lindsay's sudden probing question caught Hailey off guard, and she frowned in response to the intrusion. After a thoughtful pause, Hailey finally responded, choosing her words carefully.

'Yes,' Hailey took a more deliberate sip of her drink, suddenly finding some inexplicable comfort in its taste, 'he was. He was just as abusive.'

Lindsay's response was direct and uncompromising. 'I can't believe social services didn't intervene earlier if you were in danger.'

As Hailey contemplated her answer, she drained her glass, allowing the liquid to provide a momentary buffer. She made no protest as Lindsay promptly refilled her glass.

'I don't think it was deliberate, it was more about them not being able to handle their own issues.'

'You don't have to defend them, Hailey.'

Hailey was taken aback. 'I'm not.'

While she knew her foster parents wouldn't win a Parents-of-the-Year award, she knew many kids in foster care whose parents did much worse things to them she couldn't even bring herself to talk about.

'Do you mind me asking how they abused you?'

As Hailey took another sip of her drink, she felt a familiar stinging sensation behind her eyes, a sign that these memories and emotions were far from distant or forgotten.

'There wasn't one thing in particular. My home life was chaotic and unpredictable, which was tough.'

As the conversation flowed, Hailey couldn't help but feel a subtle shift in Lindsay's questions. They began to delve deeper, subtly probing into Hailey's past and experiences. Hailey navigated the enquiries with a mixture of caution and honesty, offering glimpses into her life while keeping certain aspects guarded.

Hailey placed her hand over her glass when Lindsay attempted to refill it again.

Hailey's words were slightly slurred. 'I think I've had enough.'

Somehow, they had managed to get through two bottles of wine within the span of their meal.

'All right, I'll get the bill,' Lindsay said, signalling to the waiter to bring it over.

'Thank you for joining me for lunch, Hailey. It's been very insightful.'

'No, thank you. It was lovely.'

The journey back home was a blur, and as soon as

Hailey managed to step into her bedroom, she collapsed onto her bed, her vision spinning out of control.

I'm never drinking again.

Chapter Twenty-Two

'Seriously, I can't believe you got Hailey drunk!'
'Don't be so dramatic. We had a few glasses with our lunch. It's not my fault she's a lightweight,' Lindsay said.

Sasha grabbed a bottle of water from the fridge. 'You know she's throwing her guts up?'

'Good, it'll make her feel better.'

'You really don't care about anyone, do you?'

Lindsay's response was a roll of her eyes, a gesture that spoke volumes of her attitude.

'Come on, don't act like I forced her to drink. She made her own choices.'

'I just don't get why you're so careless about things that affect people.'

Lindsay's shoulders shrugged indifferently. 'Every action has a consequence, and the sooner you realise that, the better.'

As the weight of her words lingered, it was clear that the conversation had only scratched the surface of deeper emotions and dynamics between them.

Sasha made her way back upstairs to the bathroom. Upon entering, Hailey's face, pale and flushed, turned towards her.

'Oh god, I feel so rough,' Hailey groaned.

Sasha knelt down beside her, tenderly brushing

the hair away from her face. 'Just try and relax. It'll pass.'

Hailey turned back to the toilet bowl and continued to retch, her hand gripping the edges for support. Sasha rubbed Hailey's back in a soothing rhythm until, after what seemed like an eternity, she finally leaned back, her breathing ragged.

'Here, rinse your mouth and drink some. You'll feel a bit better,' Sasha said, guiding the bottle of water to Hailey's lips.

'You're a lifesaver.'

'Well, someone's got to be.'

'I can't believe you're seeing me like this.'

Sasha grinned and wiggled her eyebrows. 'I've seen you in more compromising positions.'

Hailey gave a weak laugh. 'That's true.'

'Come on. Let's get you cleaned up and back to bed.'

With Hailey leaning against her, Sasha gently helped her to her feet and led her over to the sink, where Hailey splashed water on her face and brushed her teeth.

'I'm gonna run to the chemist and get you an electrolyte drink,' Sasha said.

'Don't be silly. I'll be fine.'

'As gorgeous as you are, at this moment in time, you look anything but fine.'

'I really wish you wouldn't make a fuss,' Hailey said once she was back in bed.

'Shh.' Sasha leaned in and kissed her on the lips. 'I want to, so let me. Besides, I can take Chloe for a walk in the buggy.'

'It's already starting to get dark and—'

'And the shop is five minutes away. I promise, I'll steer clear of alleyways.'

Sasha was soon on her way, singing lullabies to Chloe as they walked towards the end of the road. In the distance, under the dim glow of a street lamp, Sasha spotted a figure in a dark hoodie. A shiver of unease crawled up her spine. The figure seemed oddly familiar. She tried to shake off the sensation, attributing it to the dim light and her imagination playing tricks.

As she neared the shop, her unease only grew. The man was still there, loitering by the entrance, seemingly focused on her. Sasha's mind raced, memories resurfacing of having seen him before, lurking in the shadows during her walk home from her aunt's house.

Panic stirred within her, urging her to turn back, but she swallowed it down, her grip tightening on the handle of Chloe's buggy.

With every step she took, the distance between her and the man seemed to shrink. Adrenaline surged through Sasha's veins, urging her to act. In an instant, she made her decision.

As she turned to leave, she saw the man's movement out of the corner of her eye. He was advancing towards her with purpose, and Sasha's heart pounded in her chest. Without hesitation, she reached down and swiftly lifted Chloe out of the buggy. She held her close, her eyes never leaving the stranger as she broke into a run, her breath coming out in ragged gasps as she sprinted towards her house.

As she burst through the front door, breathless and terrified, Josh appeared in the hallway, alarm written across his face.

'Sasha, what happened?'

Tears welled up in Sasha's eyes as she struggled to catch her breath.

'There was a man … He was following me … I think he was going to …' Her voice trembled, the words catching in her throat.

Josh's face darkened with anger as he took Chloe from her arms. 'Are you all right? Did he hurt you?'

Sasha shook her head, her voice still shaky. 'No, I managed to get away.'

Just then, Hailey descended the stairs, her expression shifting from confusion to worry as she saw Sasha's distress.

'What's going on?'

Sasha's voice cracked as she recounted the terrifying encounter. Hailey immediately moved closer, wrapping her arms around her.

'He looked like that man from the other day.'

'What man?' Josh asked. 'What're you talking about?'

'Someone was following me on my way back from Aunt Jo's.'

'Why am I only hearing about this now?'

'Because I didn't want to worry you.'

'I think we should call the police,' Hailey suggested, her voice determined.

'The police? What's happened?'

All eyes turned to Lindsay who had made her way down the hallway to join them.

'Someone followed Sasha,' Hailey said.

'Followed you? For what?'

Sasha looked at her with widened eyes. 'What the hell does that mean? How would I know why some creep—'

'It's not just some creep though, is it? You've seen him before.' Hailey moved towards the staircase. 'I'm going to get my phone. I'm calling the police.'

'Can you all cool your jets for a minute? Why are you calling the police? Just to tell them someone followed her down the road?' Lindsay's voice sliced through the hallway, thick with scepticism. 'I've got a very important meeting with my agent tomorrow; I really don't need this drama.'

'Mum, he didn't follow me, he chased me.' Sasha's words trembled, the memory of the chase still fresh in her mind.

'Oh, make up your mind.' Lindsay's tone dripped with impatience.

'I was the one who said she was followed. And I think we should call the police.' Hailey's voice held a note of determination, a contrast to Lindsay's dismissive demeanour.

'Hailey, if anyone is going to make decisions in this house, it will be between me and my husband. So, please, don't overstep our boundaries.'

Sasha retrieved her phone from her pocket, a surge of anger fuelling her actions. 'It's not your life in danger, so as usual, you don't give a fuck.'

Lindsay's jaw hung open, shock rendering her momentarily speechless. As Sasha dialled the number for the police, Lindsay's incredulous stare burned into her.

'The police, please.' Sasha's voice remained resolute, a testament to her unwavering determination. 'I want to report a man who was going to attack me.'

As the details tumbled from Sasha's lips, her fingers trembled. When the call ended, she disconnected with a heavy sigh.

'They're sending someone round. I'll be in my room until they arrive,' she said. Without another word, she made her way upstairs, Hailey close by.

Inside her room, Sasha exhaled, releasing the pent-up emotions that had been swirling within her.

'I seriously think that woman won't be happy until I'm dead.'

Hailey's arms enveloped Sasha, offering a reassuring embrace. 'Don't be silly. She's probably just in shock.'

Sasha's laugh was bitter. 'Did she look like she was in shock to you?'

'Well, not exactly, but people react in different ways …'

'Can we not talk about her anymore, please?'

Within an hour, the echoing chime of the doorbell punctuated the air. As the sound dissipated, the blend of Lindsay's voice and the authoritative tone of the officer floated upstairs. Reacting swiftly, Sasha's determination flared, propelling her out of bed and down the stairs before Lindsay could dismiss the situation as an overreaction.

'Are you Sasha?' The officer's question was directed at her, her gaze steady as she spoke.

Sasha nodded.

'Do you mind if we come in?'

Lindsay stepped aside, allowing the officers to enter. In the kitchen, the female officer took a moment, waiting until they were all seated before she began.

'So, can you tell me exactly what happened?'

Sasha recounted the earlier events. 'But this isn't the first time I've seen him.'

The officer's eyebrows lifted slightly. 'Where do you think you've seen him before?'

'When I was on my way back home from my aunt's house a few days ago.'

'Okay. So, you said he wore a hoodie. Did you manage to see any of his features at all? His ethnicity? Facial hair?'

Sasha's mind raced back to the encounter, attempting to recall any detail she could.

'He was white, in his twenties. The thing that really stood out was his build, he was unnaturally thin.'

'Do you recall what he was wearing?'

'Jeans, tight ones, and an oversized hoodie.'

'Did he say anything to you?'

Sasha's brows furrowed as she searched her memory. Had he spoken to her? After a moment's consideration, she shook her head. Fear had made her deaf to any potential words.

'Could this be a friend you know, someone you're familiar with from university or the neighbourhood?'

Again, Sasha shook her head. 'I would definitely have recognized their body frame.'

The officer smiled. 'Okay, Sasha, you've done great. We'll have patrol cars in the area tonight, keeping an eye out for anyone matching your description.'

'And what happens if you don't find him?'

The officer's silence held its own weight, speaking volumes that words couldn't convey.

Chapter Twenty-Three

After Lindsay made the announcement about her upcoming biography, Emily, her agent, had been relentless in pestering Lindsay for chapter outlines. Emily wanted to get an idea of Lindsay's writing plans, which had pushed Lindsay to bring an idea that had been brewing in her mind to its full fruition. Glancing at the clock, Lindsay noted that she had time to root around in Hailey's room before she returned from work.

Stepping into Hailey's room, Lindsay's eyes darted around, taking in the surprisingly tidy space. For a teenager, Hailey was impressively organised, with everything in its place. Lindsay began to methodically open cupboards, taking care to leave no trace of her search. She was on a quest for clues, anything that could shed light on Hailey's past and help Lindsay gain a clearer understanding of her background. She hoped to find pictures of previous residences, old friends, or any memorabilia that could piece together Hailey's history. Among the items she discovered was a box tucked away in the wardrobe, filled with stacks of papers. However, upon closer examination, Lindsay realised that these documents didn't provide the insight she was hoping for. Hailey seemed to be a master of leaving minimal traces of her personal history behind.

Feeling a pang of disappointment, Lindsay closed

the wardrobe door and turned her attention to Hailey's desk. As she opened the desk drawers, her eyes were drawn to a large leather-bound diary. Could this be the key to unlocking Hailey's innermost thoughts and experiences? Noting the diary's position, Lindsay decided to take it with her to her office for further inspection.

As Lindsay delved into the pages of the diary, she quickly realised that she had stumbled upon a treasure trove of Hailey's emotions, thoughts, and life experiences. A sense of elation washed over Lindsay; she had struck gold. Every detail she needed to shape Hailey's story was right there, meticulously recorded on those pages.

What Lindsay hadn't anticipated was the extent of Hailey's reflections on Sasha, and a sly grin crept onto her face.

That little minx.

It appeared that Hailey and Sasha had been sleeping together right under her nose, and Lindsay had been completely oblivious. Sasha's sexual orientation held no surprise for Lindsay; she had long sensed it. However, she had deliberately chosen not to address it, opting to let Sasha grapple with her own secrets. Lindsay relished the idea that she held this knowledge over Sasha, a leverage of sorts that allowed her to manipulate the situation.

With a sense of urgency, Lindsay photocopied each page of the diary.

Once the task was completed, Lindsay carefully returned the diary to its original place.

Suppressing a triumphant smile, she returned to her office, eager to start writing.

***

Lindsay sat perched on a sleek leather chair in her agent's office, her fingers drumming nervously on her thigh. The office exuded an air of sophistication, its walls adorned with framed book covers and shelves brimming with meticulously organized volumes. A large wooden desk dominated the centre of the room, piled with manuscripts and notes, a testament to the agent's dedication. Behind the desk, floor-to-ceiling windows showcased a panoramic view of the city below. As Lindsay's gaze flitted around the room, her anticipation was replaced by a sense of unease. The quiet tick of a clock on the wall seemed to underscore the importance of the meeting, and she fidgeted in her seat, waiting for her agent to arrive.

The door to her office swung open, and Emily walked in with a warm smile.

Emily was a petite woman with expressive eyes that often revealed her emotions before her words did. Today, those eyes were shining with a sense of excitement that mirrored Lindsay's own.

'Lindsay,' Emily greeted, her voice tinged with enthusiasm. 'I couldn't wait to see you. I've been reading the chapters you sent over, and I have to say, I'm absolutely blown away.'

Lindsay's heart skipped a beat, her nervousness

momentarily forgotten. 'You have? I mean, thank you, Emily. I put a lot into those chapters.'

Emily pulled up a chair and sat down, her eyes never leaving Lindsay's. 'You've done more than put a lot into them, Lindsay. These chapters are exceptional. They're raw, emotional, and so beautifully written. I haven't been this moved by a manuscript in a long time.'

A rush of emotion surged through Lindsay, both relief and sheer elation. 'I'm so glad to hear that, Emily. I've been pouring my heart into it.'

Emily leaned forward, her voice earnest. 'Lindsay, I want you to know that what you've written here is going to be a number-one bestseller. The depth of emotion, the raw honesty of your past – it's nothing short of brilliant.'

Lindsay's eyes glistened with unshed tears as she absorbed Emily's words. Validation and pride swelled within her, a sense of accomplishment that surpassed her wildest dreams. 'Thank you. That means the world to me.'

Emily's smile was genuine, her excitement infectious. 'No, thank *you*. This memoir has the potential to touch so many lives, to resonate with readers. I can already envision the accolades and the recognition it will receive.'

Lindsay's heart soared, her mind racing with possibilities. 'I can't believe it. To think that my words could have such an impact …'

'They will,' Emily assured her, her voice unwavering. 'Lindsay, you've created something truly special here.'

As they continued to discuss the manuscript, Lindsay revelled in the praise and recognition, her confidence as a writer bolstered by Emily's unwavering belief in her work.

As the meeting concluded, Emily rose from her chair, her gaze fixed on Lindsay. 'I can't wait to see this memoir in print. It's going to be a game-changer.'

Lindsay stood, her heart full, and extended her hand to Emily. 'Thank you. You've given me the motivation and inspiration to keep pushing forward.'

Emily clasped Lindsay's hand with a firm grip. 'Remember this feeling, Lindsay. You have an incredible gift, and the world is about to discover it.'

Chapter Twenty-Four

Hailey sat in her car, her gaze fixed on the bustling entrance of the university building. Spotting Sasha emerging from the crowd, she gave a quick blast of her horn, catching Sasha's attention. A grin lit up Sasha's face, and without hesitation, she excused herself from her group of friends and dashed towards the car. Moments later, the door swung open, and Sasha slid into the passenger seat, her breath coming in soft gasps from her sprint.

'What are you doing here?'

Hailey leaned in, capturing Sasha's lips in a quick and affectionate kiss. 'Surprising you.'

'Well, you definitely succeeded.'

Hailey started the engine and pulled away from the kerb. 'Buckle up, we're about to embark on a mysterious journey.'

Sasha complied, fastening her seatbelt and throwing Hailey a sidelong glance. 'You really know how to keep me on my toes.'

'Life's more exciting that way.'

Navigating through familiar streets, Hailey eventually pulled up outside an ice cream parlour. Switching off the engine, she turned to Sasha.

'Welcome to surprise number two.'

'Oooh, ice cream? I feel like a kid again.'

They entered the shop and, after ordering their ice creams, found a secluded corner to settle in.

'How are you doing today? You were gone before I woke up this morning,' Hailey said.

'Yeah, I figured it was best to escape before my mum and I ended up in another showdown.'

'Very sensible of you.'

'I thought so.' Sasha took a deliberate lick of her ice cream, her gaze locked onto Hailey's.

Hailey's brows furrowed. 'Don't do that.'

Sasha gave another seductive lick of the ice cream, her eyes never leaving Hailey's. 'Why not?' she said, feigning innocence.

Hailey's voice dropped a little lower, filled with both desire and warning. 'Because if you keep that up, I won't be able to control myself.'

Sasha's laughter rang out, light and carefree. 'I won't be the one complaining, believe me.'

'Remind me to put ice cream on the list next time we check into a hotel,' Sasha said, her lips curling into a mischievous smile.

'And whipped cream.'

'You're such a tease.'

Hailey reached across the table to clasp Sasha's hand. 'In all seriousness, I'm really worried about this hoodie guy and what he's capable of.'

'Me too.'

Hailey hesitated briefly, her voice lowering. 'I think I'm starting to see what you mean about your mum. She was well out of order yesterday. If you were my daughter, I would've been frantic.'

Sasha let out a resigned sigh. 'That's my mum for you.'

Hailey's grip on Sasha's hand tightened. 'So … I thought if your mum doesn't give a damn about you, I'm going to drop you off and pick you up from uni every day.'

'Don't be silly. You've got to work. You can't be my personal bodyguard.'

'I'd rather know you were safe than keep my job.'

A tender smile played on Sasha's lips as she squeezed Hailey's hand. 'Thank you.'

'There's no need to thank me.'

'Yeah, there is.' Sasha's gaze held Hailey's, sincerity shining in her eyes. 'Not only for caring about me but for being the best thing that's ever happened in my life.'

Hailey leaned over and pressed a soft kiss to Sasha's lips.

'Likewise,' Hailey said. 'How about one more kiss to seal the deal?'

'You know, you're making it really hard for me to focus on anything other than you.'

'Well, maybe that's the plan.'

Sasha playfully swatted her arm. 'Hailey!'

They made small talk while they finished their ice creams. Noting Sasha kept checking her phone, Hailey knew it was time to call it a day.

'Ready to head home?' Hailey asked, her thumb gently caressing Sasha's hand.

Sasha nodded, a frustrated sigh escaping her lips. 'Yeah, if we must.'

For the first time, Hailey knew exactly how Sasha felt. She was dreading returning to what she had once thought was a safe haven – which was now tainted and no longer the place she had believed it to be.

Chapter Twenty-Five

Days had passed since Lindsay's meeting with her agent, and though she had been on a high like no other, today Lindsay found herself sinking back into her chair, her temples throbbing as she closed her eyes and inhaled a deep breath. What had she expected? That her fantastical story would fly under the radar and go unnoticed? She didn't really know, but what she hadn't been expecting was the email she'd received an hour earlier: an invite to appear on a prominent radio talk show. She had read the message with trepidation. While the opportunity promised to cast a spotlight on her new book, there was an underlying anxiety, a shadowy fear that clung to her like a dark cloud. What if Hailey heard the interview?

The room seemed to close in on her as she stood up and began pacing the floor. The question lingered: Should she accept? It was nine a.m. The interview was at two p.m., leaving her five hours to decide. A sudden gap in the show's line-up had prompted Emily, who was friends with the show's producer, to suggest Lindsay fill the void. Emily had insisted that this was Lindsay's chance to ascend to new heights in her career, so declining seemed almost like an impossible choice; it would only raise questions and arouse suspicion.

Returning to her computer, Lindsay clicked on

the reply button, her fingers moving swiftly across the keyboard.

Hi Sue,

Absolutely, count me in! I'm truly excited about the opportunity and can't wait to speak!

Warm regards,

Lindsay
X

She quickly pressed the send button before she could change her mind.

Taking a deep breath, Lindsay reassured herself that if things took an awkward turn or delved into territories she wished to avoid, she could always blame technical glitches and disconnect the call. It wasn't the first time she had employed this tactic, and it seemed like a safety net she could fall back on.

As the deadline loomed, Lindsay found herself in the kitchen, a glass of chilled wine within arm's reach. She had a quick conversation with the producer to iron out the last-minute details, and then the moment arrived – she was live on air.

The host's introduction was a familiar cadence of accolades, listing Lindsay's literary achievements and lauding her as a source of inspiration for struggling parents. The expected questions came: the routine enquiries about her writing process, her muses, and her journey to becoming an author. Lindsay answered them all with a practised eloquence, years of experience shaping her responses.

However, a surprise came out of nowhere, catching her off guard: a question she hadn't rehearsed, hadn't prepared for. It was a query about the real-life experiences that were enabling her to write her memoir.

'It sounds like your biography comes from a deeply personal place. Can you share a specific instance that inspired you?'

Lindsay's throat constricted, and her palms grew damp as her mind raced to formulate an answer. She drained her wine before she began to recount fragments of Hailey's life that she had moulded into her narrative. The host seemed to be captivated, hanging onto her every word.

Once the interview concluded, Lindsay disconnected the call and poured herself another glass of wine.

I think I did pretty well. All that worrying was for nothing.

Though in an ebullient mood, a shadow loomed, a persistent fear that gnawed at her. The fear of Hailey discovering the truth. How long could she keep up the façade before it all came crashing down?

Chapter Twenty-Six

Sasha leaned against the doorway of the living room, her voice tentative.

'Have you spoken to Dad today?'

Lindsay's eyes remained fixed on her computer screen. 'No.'

'I tried calling him, but his phone's switched off.'

'What'd you want him for?' Lindsay's tone was detached, uninterested.

'Nothing that can't wait,' Sasha said, opting not to delve into the details of her reasons.

She had no intention of questioning her mother about her father's recent withdrawal into his own world. The atmosphere in the house had changed since her parents had returned from the event at the bookshop; it felt more toxic, if that was even possible.

'I forgot to ask you how your meeting with your agent went?' Sasha continued, her attempt at conversation genuine.

Lindsay's lips formed a hint of a smile, though the sarcasm in her voice was unmistakable. 'It went well, thanks for asking.'

'Sorry, but you don't normally like me talking about your new books. That's why I didn't ask.'

She couldn't help but recall the countless times she'd tried to connect with her mother through discussions about her work, only to be met with a dismissive attitude.

Despite this, Sasha had devoured every single one of Lindsay's books, each time emerging with a sense of amazement that someone so insightful could be so distant.

'If you must know, she loved the concept of my work,' Lindsay said, her tone softening slightly.

'What's it about?'

'It's personal,' Lindsay's response was guarded, a wall between them.

Sasha couldn't help but smile wryly. 'It can't be that personal, considering you've shared it with a stranger.'

'Emily is not a stranger. She also has my back at all times.'

'Are you saying that I don't?'

Lindsay's response was cryptic. 'I do wonder sometimes.'

An uncomfortable silence stretched between them, the room filled only with the sound of Lindsay's fingers tapping away at the keyboard.

'I'm sorry you feel that way, Mum,' Sasha said, her voice tinged with sadness.

Lindsay turned to her, her eyes blinking slowly as if her thoughts were struggling to catch up with the delayed revelation. The tension in the room seemed to thicken, the unspoken emotions lingering in the air.

'And I'm sorry I brought an emotionally inept child into the world.' Lindsay's words dripped with a bitter edge, her voice laced with an undercurrent of disdain.

Sasha's frown deepened. 'What does that mean?'

Lindsay's lips curved into a smirk, her gaze unwavering. 'You're eighteen years old and you still haven't managed to snag yourself a boyfriend, even one that would date you for pity sex.'

The comment landed like a punch in the gut, a painful reminder of Lindsay's penchant for using Sasha's vulnerabilities as ammunition. Sasha's cheeks burned with anger. Her mother's ability to wound with her words was truly remarkable.

'I … uh …' Sasha stammered, her voice betraying her surprise at the unexpected attack.

Lindsay stood up and walked over to the window. Her smile held a hint of smugness. 'Maybe you should ask Hailey for some tips. I'm sure she has no problem attracting men.'

A sudden crash broke the uneasy silence. The sound of shattering glass filled the room as a brick hurtled through the window, scattering shards everywhere. Sasha and Lindsay instinctively ducked, their hands covering their heads as fragments of glass rained down around them. The impact was jarring, a shockwave that rippled through the room.

Sasha's heart pounded in her chest, fear coursing through her veins. Her pulse raced as she glanced around, eyes wide and searching. With a surge of adrenaline, Sasha pushed herself up from the floor and rushed to the window.

Through the chaos of broken glass and the disarray of the room, she caught a fleeting glimpse of a figure disappearing down the street. A man in a hoodie, the same unnaturally thin man she had encountered before. The sight sent a chill down her spine, a wave of dread crashing over her.

'Mum, it's him!' Sasha's voice trembled as she stared at the retreating figure.

Lindsay, still on the floor, looked up at Sasha, her eyes wide with shock.

Sasha's fingers fumbled for her phone, her hands shaking as she dialled for the police. Her voice trembled as she gave the dispatcher their address and explained what had just happened. The words spilled out in a rush, fear driving her.

As they waited for the police to arrive, Sasha's trembling hands reached for her phone again. This time she called Hailey.

'Hey, not surprisingly, I was just thinking about—' Hailey's said.

'H-Hailey' – Sasha's voice wavered – 'you won't believe what just happened.'

'Sasha, what's wrong? Are you okay?'

'A brick … a brick was thrown through the window.' Sasha's voice cracked, tears threatening to spill over.

'What? Are you serious? Are you okay?'

'I'm fine, but … it's him, Hailey. The man in the hoodie.'

Hailey's silence spoke volumes, the gravity of the situation sinking in. 'I'm on my way. I'll be there as fast as I can.'

She thanked her and hung up, her fingers still trembling. Lindsay had managed to sit up, her face pale and eyes wide.

When the police arrived and began assessing the situation, Sasha's mind raced. The man in the hoodie had escalated from lurking in the shadows to a direct attack on their home. The sense of violation was overwhelming, a feeling that safety and normalcy had been shattered along with the window.

Chapter Twenty-Seven

'Stay in a hotel and be run out of my home like a scared mouse? Never!'

Lindsay's voice was like a sharp blade cutting through the subdued atmosphere.

The suggestion from the police to stay at a hotel until the shattered window was repaired had ignited a wave of conflicting emotions within the household. Hailey's gaze turned to Lindsay, who stood with arms crossed, a defiant set to her jaw.

It was no surprise that Lindsay adamantly declared she wouldn't be chased out of her own home for anyone. Josh, ever the peacemaker, stood beside her, nodding in agreement, although his gaze held a trace of uncertainty.

As the discussion unfolded, Hailey found herself trapped in a whirlwind of thoughts and emotions. She glanced at Sasha, their eyes meeting briefly, a silent exchange that spoke volumes.

'I am not staying here, and I don't care what you say,' Sasha said.

'If you want to run away like a little coward, then go, but you'll go by yourself. We're staying here, Chloe too.'

'Look, can we all calm down,' Josh said, rubbing his hand over his face. 'Let's discuss this like grown adults.'

After moments of back-and-forth deliberation, a decision was finally reached. Hailey and Sasha would spend the night at a hotel. Josh's reasoning was sensible, his words echoing in Hailey's mind as they gathered their belongings.

'It's just for one night, to let things cool down.'

Hailey knew he meant well, but the frustration had already begun to mount.

As they made their way to the hotel, Hailey's thoughts were a tempest of anger and resentment. Lindsay's stubbornness irked her. It wasn't about being chased out; it was about ensuring their safety. The fact that Lindsay couldn't see beyond her pride stung like a thorn. *Selfish*, Hailey thought, unable to shake off the feeling.

Josh's compliance in Lindsay's decision didn't sit well with Hailey either. She had always admired his level-headedness, but right now, it felt like he was being a wet blanket, dampening any attempts to address the situation head-on. The urge to shake some sense into him nagged at her, but she had held her tongue, her focus on getting through the evening.

In the hotel lobby, Sasha's fingers tapped nervously on the counter.

'We're here to check in. The reservation is under Josh Miller.'

The hotel receptionist smiled warmly, her fingers dancing across the keyboard. 'Ah, yes. I see your reservation here. One double room for one night. Is that correct?'

Sasha nodded, offering a faint smile. 'Yes, that's right.'

When they entered their hotel room, Hailey reached for Sasha's hand.

'Sasha, I'm scared for you. What if this person is targeting you?'

Sasha's eyes glistened with unshed tears. 'I don't know, Hailey. I don't even know who would want to mess with my mind like this.'

Hailey cupped Sasha's cheek in her hand. 'At least we're safe here. Let's just focus on that tonight.'

They stood there for a moment, their foreheads pressed together, seeking solace in the closeness they shared. Eventually, they moved towards the bed and lay down, Sasha nestling into the crook of Hailey's arm.

'I can't help but think, what if the police are wrong and this isn't just some random attack. What if that brick was meant for me?' Sasha said.

'The police said it's very unlikely. It's probably like they said, some idiot who's got nothing better to do with their time.'

Sasha's expression was pained, her vulnerability laid bare. 'This feels personal. What if Chloe had been home? She could've been hurt.'

'Well, she wasn't. You've got to stop thinking like that.'

'You weren't there. You didn't feel how scary it was.'

Hailey refrained from telling Sasha she had experienced a lot worse than a brick being thrown through a window. Much, much worse, but this wasn't about her. It was about Sasha, and her feelings of being afraid were valid.

Hailey brushed her fingers against Sasha's cheek, her touch gentle. 'I know. All I'm saying is that you can't let fear control you. Imagine if we'd been too scared to admit our feelings for each other. Look at what we would've missed out on.'

Sasha shifted, pulling Hailey closer until their bodies were pressed together, their hearts beating in sync.

'I don't even want to think about it.'

Chapter Twenty-Eight

Jo's smile couldn't fully mask the concern that flashed in her eyes as Sasha and Hailey followed her into the living room.

'Sasha, if I caught the bastard, I'd …' Her voice faltered as she glanced over at Hailey. 'I'm sorry about my language, but the thought of someone trying to harm Sasha makes my blood boil.'

'No need to apologise. I feel exactly the same way,' Hailey said.

They all took a seat on the sofa and Jo directed her attention at Sasha.

'And you've no idea who this stalker could be?'

Sasha's fingers instinctively found their way to the back of her neck, probing the taut muscles.

'Nope. I've wracked my brain trying to think if I've upset anyone recently or looked at them the wrong way, but nothing comes to mind.'

Jo turned to Hailey. 'Look, I don't want you to take this the wrong way, but—'

'It's okay, I've had the same thought myself. Is it someone from my past, but the truth is no one knows where I live.'

'At least you don't think they do,' Jo said.

A soft exhale escaped Hailey's lips. 'Okay, say it was someone I knew. It doesn't add up though, does it? If they were after me, they'd wait until I was around.

Following Sasha when I'm not there … it doesn't make sense.'

'Yeah, you're right,' Sasha said.

Sasha felt as if she had been ensnared in an unending nightmare, a relentless loop she couldn't escape from. How had her life shifted so drastically, transitioning from a semblance of normalcy to this intricate web of uncertainty and fear?

'I'm just not buying that some random stranger just happened to take a fancy to you,' Jo said.

'Why not? Hailey did.'

Laughter broke out, easing the tension.

'That's true,' Hailey said.

Suddenly, Sasha's laughter tapered off, her voice taking on a more serious tone. 'What if …'

'What is it?' Hailey and Jo said in unison.

The air seemed to hold a moment of suspended anticipation, as if Sasha's thoughts were on the verge of unveiling a revelation.

'This isn't about me at all,' Sasha finally said. 'What if all this has to do with my mum?'

The room seemed to hold its breath, the weight of Sasha's words hanging in the air.

Sasha turned to Jo, whose complexion had visibly paled.

'Oh god, sorry. I didn't mean to get you all worried about my mum,' Sasha quickly interjected, a touch of regret in her voice. 'It's just a thought.'

'But it's actually a pretty solid one,' Hailey said, her voice gaining momentum as she explained her thoughts. 'I mean, if you really think about it, it makes sense. All it takes is some guy reading one of Lindsay's books and misinterpreting things. I've read books before, you know, about stuff like foster care, and sometimes I'm tempted to contact the authors and ask them if they really understand what they're talking about. It's like they're trying to tackle serious issues, but it comes across as unrealistic and insensitive.'

Sasha felt a sense of relief that they were actually getting somewhere.

'What do you think, Aunt Jo?'

Jo's response was measured, her brows furrowing as she considered the notion.

'I think … it's a possibility. But how can you prove it?'

'I guess we can't really, but maybe Lindsay could do something like post a statement on her website or social media. You know, address the issues people might have with her work.'

'There's no point in even asking. She'd never do that,' Sasha said.

'She might,' Hailey said, her optimism unwavering.

Jo's eyes held a knowing look, a hint of fond exasperation in her expression. 'I'm with Sasha on this one. You don't know Lindsay.'

Hailey's forehead creased in curiosity. 'Oh?'

'If—'

Sasha smoothly interjected, redirecting the conversation. 'Would you mind if I made us a sandwich? We've barely eaten today.'

'Sure, I'll make it,' Jo offered.

'I'll help,' Sasha said, following her into the kitchen. 'Sorry for cutting you off. It's just that Hailey has only had a glimpse of what Mum is capable of. I'm hoping she'll be long gone before she sees her true colours.'

'I see.' Jo reached into the fridge to retrieve the ham and tomatoes.

'Mum puts on a good game, especially in front of Hailey.'

Jo switched the kettle on and took three cups out the cupboard. 'And how are things between you and your mum?'

Sasha let out a sigh. 'As messed up as ever. We had a pretty intense conversation yesterday. I stupidly tried to do some mother-daughter bonding thing but it turned nasty as usual. I'm sick of hoping things will change between us.'

'It's hard when you're yearning for a connection that's proving elusive.'

'Tell me about it.' Sasha gave a rueful smile. 'Me being polite by asking about her work turned into her reacting with her usual charm. She belittled my feelings, and told me I couldn't even get a pity shag.'

Jo gasped. 'She really said that?'

'Yep.'

Jo's hand reached out and settled gently on Sasha's forearm. 'It sounds like things have become even more strained between you two.'

Sasha nodded, her gaze dropping to the ground.

'Yeah, and what's worse is that when she made that comment, I nearly told her I was gay.'

Jo took a loaf of bread out the cupboard and handed it to Sasha. 'I advised you years ago to tell her and just let the cards fall where they may. You shouldn't have to be afraid to be who you are.'

'I don't have an issue with being gay, I have an issue with my mum using it against me. I dread to think how she'll react when I eventually tell her.'

'So,' Jo said, a small smile playing on her lips. 'I take it you two have moved forward in your relationship since I last saw you?'

Sasha grinned as Jo washed the tomatoes and began slicing them. 'Yeah, we've taken some steps forward.'

'That's good.'

Sasha spread butter across the slices of bread as she added, 'It's been good, really good. In fact, if it wasn't for all this stalker drama, I would say for the first time in my life, everything is perfect.'

Jo's gaze was gentle as she observed her. 'I'm glad to hear that. It'll be wedding bells next.'

Sasha's cheeks flushed faintly as she concentrated on layering the sandwich. 'You never know, Aunt Jo. You never know.'

Chapter Twenty-Nine

Lindsay was properly drunk for the first time in months. Not her usual tipsy state, but so intoxicated that her movements were unsteady and her speech slurred. She leaned against the kitchen worktop for support, her hand gripping the edge as she swayed slightly. The scent of alcohol permeated the air around her. The memories she'd been desperately trying to bury were resurfacing with a vengeance. Images of the past, mistakes she couldn't undo, were haunting her. She had built her life on layers of secrets, carefully crafted to present a picture of normalcy. But that façade was cracking, and she felt like the walls were closing in on her.

As she staggered into the living room, the empty wine glass clutched in her hand, she sank onto the sofa. Her breath came in ragged bursts and tears welled in her eyes. She had always managed to keep her emotions in check, to play the part of the composed and put-together woman. But tonight, the weight of her choices was crushing her.

The familiar sound of keys being dropped onto the hallway table echoed through the house, making her jump. She wiped her tears hastily and managed to steady herself as she got to her feet. It was Josh, back from work earlier than usual.

'Hi,' he greeted her, his eyes narrowing as he

took in her dishevelled appearance.

'Hi,' she slurred, her voice heavy with the effects of alcohol.

He stepped closer, concern etched on his face. 'Lindsay, are you okay?'

'I'm fine,' she snapped, her defences rising as she tried to maintain control.

Josh sighed and ran a hand through his hair. 'Look, we can't keep avoiding this. We need to talk about it.'

Her heart raced, panic and anger surging within her. 'Talk about what?'

'The secret we've been hiding all these years.'

She felt her knees go weak, stumbling back onto the sofa, her grip on reality slipping.

'It's eating away at both of us,' Josh continued.

Lindsay's vision blurred as tears continued to stream down her cheeks. The alcohol had intensified her emotions, making her feel raw and exposed. She wanted to blame Josh, to lay their secret solely on his shoulders, but she knew deep down that she was just as culpable.

'You are going to …' she said, her voice breaking. 'Fix this. This is all your fault, you stupid bastard.'

She leaned her head back against the sofa, the leather fabric cool against her flushed skin. The room spun around her, a physical manifestation of the turmoil within her.

'We should have dealt with this years ago,' she muttered.

Josh took a seat beside her. 'I know, but we can't

change the past. We can only decide what to do now. I'll make things right this time around. I promise.'

'Just make sure you do. If this comes out, especially now, my career is finished.'

The past had finally caught up with them. It was now time to pay their dues.

Chapter Thirty

Sasha's footsteps faltered as she entered the familiar confines of her home. A sense of unease settled in her chest, a premonition of something amiss. As she walked into the living room, her heart sank at the sight that greeted her. Lindsay was waiting for her, her posture rigid and her expression inscrutable.

A knot of anxiety formed in Sasha's stomach. 'Mum, are you all right?'

Lindsay's gaze met Sasha's, bereft of the maternal warmth it should have held. 'Sit down.'

Sasha sank into a chair, her palms growing clammy. She had experienced her fair share of uncomfortable conversations with her mother, but this time, the tension was almost suffocating.

Lindsay cleared her throat, her voice uncharacteristically sombre. 'Sasha, there's something we need to discuss.'

Sasha's forehead creased in a frown. 'What is it?'

'Hailey.'

'Hailey? What about her?'

A heavy sigh escaped Lindsay's lips. 'I've been thinking about this for a while now … and I think it's for the best that Hailey moves out.'

Sasha's heart plummeted. 'What? No, Mum, you can't be serious.'

'I'm very serious, Sasha. Her presence here has

disrupted our family dynamic. It's time for things to go back to normal.'

'But this is normal, Mum. Hailey is a part of our lives now. She's not disrupting anything.'

Lindsay's tone turned icy. 'Sasha, this is my home, and I decide who lives here, not you.'

Tears welled up in Sasha's eyes. 'You don't understand. Hailey is special to me, I—'

'I couldn't care less. She's going and that's the end of it.'

Lindsay's indifference was a painful blow, her lack of empathy cutting deep.

'Please don't do this, Mum. Please.'

'Life isn't about what we want, Sasha. It's about making tough decisions for the greater good.'

Sasha's tears spilled over, her voice breaking as she pleaded, 'Can you just give it a few more days to think about it?'

'No, and that's final.'

The front door opened and closed with a thud and Hailey's voice soon echoed through the hallway.

'Hey, I'm home!'

Sasha wiped away her tears and said in a hushed voice, 'If you kick Hailey out, then I'm going with her.'

Lindsay's expression remained unchanged, her eyes cold and calculating. 'And what about Chloe?'

Sasha's breath caught in her throat, the mention of her younger sister a painful reminder of the responsibilities she bore.

'Chloe … she'll be okay. I'll make sure she's

taken care of.'

'If you leave, I will have to put Chloe up for adoption. Is that what you want?'

Sasha's heart raced, torn between her love for Hailey and her duty towards her sister.

As Hailey's footsteps drew nearer, Sasha's gaze locked with Lindsay's one final time. In that moment, she saw the void of empathy and the selfishness that defined her mother.

As Hailey entered the room, Sasha's heartache was mirrored in her tear-filled eyes.

'Is everything okay?'

'No, it isn't,' Sasha said.

She didn't have the heart to tell Hailey that she was facing an impossible choice, one that threatened to tear them apart.

Chapter Thirty-One

'I can't believe your mum's throwing me out. What have I done?' Hailey said as she paced the room, her agitation evident in every step she took.

Sasha, standing by the window, looked out aimlessly. She appeared just as shocked as Hailey felt.

'Nothing. You didn't do anything. My mum has a tendency to create stories in her head and convince herself they're true.'

Hailey sank onto the bed, burying her face in her hands. 'I knew this was too good to be true. I should've known better.'

Sasha stepped away from the window and joined Hailey, settling beside her. She wrapped her arm around Hailey's waist, pulling her close. 'I don't know what to say.'

Hailey let out a muffled laugh, devoid of humour. 'You don't have to say anything. You're not the one making me homeless.'

'I can try and talk to her again, but I doubt it will do any good. Once my mum makes up her mind, that's it.'

Hailey's eyes searched Sasha's, a glimmer of hope returning. 'What about your dad? Maybe he can talk some sense into her.'

'I wish I could say that would help, but he just agrees with whatever my mum decides. He's always been scared to stand up to her.'

Hailey's heart sank further at the realisation that the odds were stacked against her. She leaned into Sasha's embrace.

'I don't know what to do. I don't want to lose you.'

Sasha gently cupped Hailey's cheek, her thumb wiping away a stray tear.

'You won't lose me, Hailey. No matter what happens, we'll find a way to be together.'

'Do you think … could we find a place of our own? Somewhere we can live without all this drama?'

Sasha dropped her gaze.

'I take it that's a no, then.'

'It's not that simple.'

'Yes, it is,' Hailey said, grabbing Sasha's hands. 'I can work more hours to earn more money and you can get a part-time job, we—'

Sasha got to her feet. 'I can't, Hailey, no matter how much I want to.'

'Can't or won't?' Hailey said.

Suddenly the door flew open, and Lindsay walked in with a stern expression.

'Don't try to entice my daughter into leaving, Hailey. She isn't built for the kind of life you could offer her.'

Sasha's eyes narrowed. 'Were you eavesdropping?'

Lindsay's tone remained firm, undeterred by the accusation. 'No, I came up to see if Hailey's packing. I've called Christine and informed her of the situation.'

Hailey's eyebrows furrowed as she got to her

feet. 'Situation? Lindsay, if I've done something to upset you, I wish you'd tell me so I can make it right.'

'The only way you can make it right is by leaving.'

Sasha's jaw tightened, and her hands curled into fists. 'You can't just force her to leave. She hasn't got anywhere to go.'

'That's not my problem. I've done my part. I opened my home to you and treated you as if you were my own daughter, but things haven't worked out the way I thought they would.'

'Only because you won't let them,' Sasha said, tears streaming down her cheeks.

'It's okay, Sasha. I'll be fine. I'll have my stuff ready within an hour.'

Hailey walked over to the wardrobe, took out her case and started packing her clothes. 'Thank you for letting me stay, Lindsay. And I'm sorry that things have ended this way.'

'It is what it is.' Lindsay turned to walk out, before saying over her shoulder, 'Chloe needs feeding, Sasha.'

As soon as she closed the door behind her, Sasha bit her fist. 'I swear, I fucking hate that woman! All she's ever done is bring misery into my life.'

'You have a choice, you know.'

'That's the problem, I don't.'

Sasha swung the door open and left the room.

Hailey didn't know what to take from that comment, but whatever hold Lindsay had over Sasha was one that she knew she couldn't compete with.

As she folded her clothes and packed her belongings into a bag, Hailey replayed their recent conversations in her mind, searching for clues and hidden meanings.

But amidst the confusion, there was a sense of determination simmering within her. Hailey knew that whatever complicated dynamics existed between Sasha and Lindsay, she couldn't let them dictate her feelings or actions. She couldn't compete with a past she didn't fully understand. With a deep breath, she zipped up her bag and cast a final glance around the room.

Hearing a car pull up outside, Hailey went to the window to see Christine getting out of her car.

I wonder what she told her to make her drop everything and come straight here? A bunch of lies, probably.

She heard muffled voices from below and then the sound of footsteps ascending the stairs. The door opened, revealing Christine with a sad smile on her face. Unable to hold back the flood of emotions, tears streamed down Hailey's cheeks. In an instant, Christine enveloped her in a comforting hug, her hand gently smoothing Hailey's hair.

'It's okay, it's okay, I'm here,' Christine whispered reassuringly.

Hailey's sobs continued, but the embrace offered a sense of solace she desperately needed.

'I don't know what I did, Christine,' Hailey managed to choke out between sobs.

Christine's hold tightened. 'It'll be all right,' she murmured softly, her voice a soothing balm. 'Let's get out of here. Leave your car here, you can come back for it later. You aren't in any state to drive.'

Christine released Hailey from their embrace and helped her gather her belongings. As they walked past the living room, Hailey heard the sound of Sasha's muffled sobs. Her heart ached at the thought of leaving Sasha in such a state. She halted in her tracks, the need to ensure Sasha was okay pulling at her.

Just as Hailey was about to push the door open to check on Sasha, Lindsay suddenly blocked her path. Hailey's brow knitted in confusion, her concern for Sasha momentarily overshadowed.

'The front door is that way,' Lindsay said coldly.

With a heavy sigh, Hailey reluctantly turned away, her footsteps heavy as she walked the short distance to the door and pulled it closed behind her, ending yet another chapter in her life.

Chapter Thirty-Two

Sasha paced back and forth in her room, her frustration building with each step. She could feel the heat rising in her cheeks as she clenched her fists, her heart pounding in her chest. Lindsay stood in the doorway, her arms crossed, a stern expression on her face.

'You can't take my phone away,' Sasha spat out, her words dripping with defiance and resentment.

Lindsay's eyes narrowed. 'I can, and I will. I don't want you talking to Hailey again. It's for your own good.'

'I'm eighteen, not a child. I can make my own choices.'

'While you're under this roof, you'll abide—'

'Same old threat,' Sasha cut in. 'What you up to, Mum? One minute, you're forcing me to stay; the next, you're practically pushing me out. Is this about control? Because it isn't about love or protection. I bet if the house were burning down, you'd leave me to fend for myself.'

'Get a grip, Sasha. You're being dramatic.'

'Am I?'

'Yes, you are. Hailey is trouble waiting to happen.'

'You don't know Hailey, yet you're so quick to judge. You know what? She cares about me, unlike you.'

'Sasha, I'm your mother. Everything I do is to

protect you.'

Sasha scoffed. 'Protect me? The only thing I need protection from is you! You know … I think I might actually hate you.'

Lindsay's lips curled into a cold smile. 'Then I've done my job as a mother.'

'You keep telling yourself that,' she muttered under her breath.

'Get some sleep now,' Lindsay instructed. 'Your dad and I are going out early tomorrow, so you'll need to get Chloe ready.'

When don't I?

Sasha refrained from further confrontation and Lindsay left.

Getting ready for bed, Sasha felt her room turn into a cage, trapping her. Lindsay's control had always suffocated her, but this was a new level of frustration. She needed a way to reach out to Hailey. Climbing into bed, she switched off the bedside lamp.

Her mother's words echoed: 'I don't want you talking to Hailey anymore. She's a bad influence.' The memory fuelled Sasha's anger, a fire simmering beneath her skin.

Who does she think she is, telling me who I can or can't talk to?

Sasha tossed and turned, consumed by thoughts of Hailey. The house was eerily quiet, the darkness amplifying her restlessness. She couldn't shake the feeling that Hailey might be reaching out, and she was determined to get her phone back. Her resolve grew with each passing minute.

The bedside clock read 11:47 p.m. Sasha knew she had to be cautious and quiet, not wanting to wake anyone in the house. Slipping out from under the covers, her bare feet brushed against the cool wooden floor. Inhaling deeply, she cracked her bedroom door open and peered into the dimly lit hallway. All was quiet.

Sasha tiptoed down the corridor, her heart racing. Her destination was clear: her mother's office. She reached the door, held her breath, and gently turned the doorknob. The door creaked open, and she slipped inside.

The office was shrouded in shadows, the moonlight casting a faint glow through the curtains. Sasha's eyes adjusted as she made her way to the desk. She opened a drawer, fingers fumbling as she sifted through the clutter for her phone. To her dismay, it wasn't there. Her mother must have moved it.

Despite her frustration, Sasha pressed on. She noticed another drawer slightly ajar and pulled it open. Instead of her phone, a stack of neatly arranged papers met her eyes. Curiosity piqued, she pulled them out and scanned the pages. Diary entries, each page filled with handwritten words.

In the low light, she could hardly make out the words, and just as she was about to look closer, the room was suddenly flooded with light. She froze.

'What are you doing here?'

Sasha's head snapped towards the doorway, meeting Josh's gaze.

'I … I was just looking for my phone,' Sasha stammered.

Josh's eyes narrowed, his expression unreadable. 'In the middle of the night? In your mother's office?'

Sasha's mind raced for an explanation. 'Mum took my phone, and I wanted to check if she had it here.'

Josh's gaze remained fixed on her. 'Go back to bed.'

Sasha nodded, backing away from the desk. 'Please, don't tell Mum I was in here.'

He didn't reply, and Sasha slipped out of the office, her steps silent as she retreated to her room. She slid back into bed, her mind spinning with a whirlwind of thoughts. The diary entries she had glimpsed lingered in her mind.

What is she up to now?

Chapter Thirty-Three

The low hum of the engine was a stark contrast to the silence that filled the car's interior. Hailey's eyes remained fixed on the passing landscape, her mind adrift in a sea of thoughts. The separation from Sasha was hitting her hard, the reality of the situation settling in with each passing moment.

Beside her, Christine's voice cut through the quiet, drawing her attention. 'We're almost there.'

Hailey blinked, momentarily pulled from her reverie. She turned her gaze towards Christine, managing a faint smile. 'Right. And thanks for finding me a place to stay on such short notice.'

'No problem. It's unfortunate things didn't work out as expected. I had high hopes for you both.'

Hailey held back her true feelings, not wanting to vent her frustrations about Lindsay. 'Yeah, sometimes things just don't fit, I guess.'

The car came to a stop, and Hailey's eyes moved to the building ahead of them. It was a run-down hostel that seemed to have seen better days.

Christine turned towards Hailey. 'It's not exactly a five-star, but I did my best given the circumstances. I'll make some calls tomorrow and see if we can find you a better place.'

Hailey offered a wry smile. 'I've slept in worse places. As long as there are no creepy crawlies, I'll manage.'

'Things will get better, you know. Life has its ups and downs.'

'Yeah, well, my life seems to be one long rollercoaster of downs lately.'

'I wish I had your resilience when I was your age. My life would have been so different.'

'You look like you've done good from where I'm sitting.'

'It took a lot of hard work to get here, and I'm still not complete.'

Christine turned off the engine. 'Anyway, that's enough of my boring life story.'

As Christine spoke, Hailey's gaze remained fixed on the hostel. The reality of the situation was sinking in. She was alone. Again.

I wish Sasha could be here with me.

Turning to Christine, she hesitated before speaking. 'Could you … would it be okay if you stayed with me for a little while? I'm not sure I want to be alone right now.'

Exiting the car, they retrieved Hailey's case from the boot and began making their way to the hostel's entrance. The closer they got, the more their surroundings revealed their less-than-ideal nature. The stench of alcohol and urine was overpowering, loud music emanated from open windows, and a scuffle was unfolding in the lobby.

I've stepped into a nightmare.

Just as Hailey was about to push open the entrance door, she felt Christine's grip on her arm tighten. She turned to face her.

'What's wrong?'

'I can't leave you here. You're coming home with me.'

Her unexpected words caused Hailey to buckle at the knees. Christine had a knack of offering her a lifeline when she needed it most. They made their way back to the car and were soon pulling up outside Christine's home. The detached modern house was a stark contrast to the vision of hell they'd left behind.

Once inside, Christine led Hailey down a flight of stairs to the basement, where a spacious room awaited her. It had its own bathroom and a small living area, providing a sense of privacy.

'This ... this is incredible.'

'I'm glad you like it, Hailey. You can stay until you get on your feet.'

Tears welled in Hailey's eyes. 'Christine. You're being so kind to me, and I don't know how to repay you.'

Christine gave a small shake of her head. 'You don't need to repay me. You don't owe me anything. I'll let you settle in.'

Hailey sat on her bed and took out her phone. Snapping several pictures of her new space, she sent them to Sasha with a smiling emoji.

One tick appeared on the message. Hailey waited for the second one to materialize. Five minutes later, it was still one tick. Another hour passed with no change.

I hope she's all right. I'm getting worried now.

She sighed, her finger hovering over her

phone's screen as she typed out another message.

Hey, I really want to talk. Please reply when you can.

Hailey desperately willed her phone to light up with a notification. She stared at the screen intently, but it remained dark.

Just then, a soft knock on her door interrupted her thoughts. 'Come in.'

Christine walked in, holding a pizza box. 'I brought your favourite pizza. I know it's late but I figured you might be hungry.'

Hailey chuckled. 'You're a mind reader. I'm starving, actually.'

'Well, I'm hungry too,' Christine admitted with a smile as she sat on the bed and opened the pizza box. They ate in companionable silence for a few minutes.

Between bites, Hailey shared her concern. 'I messaged Sasha, but she hasn't replied yet. I'm not sure what to do.'

'Well, before you label me as old, have you tried giving her a call?' Christine suggested.

Hailey slapped her forehead lightly. 'I can't believe I didn't think of that.'

Putting her pizza slice back in the box, Hailey dialled Sasha's number. To her disappointment, it went straight to voicemail. 'Her phone's switched off.'

'That explains why she hasn't responded. Don't worry too much,' Christine reassured her.

Hailey picked up her pizza slice again. 'You know, I feel really safe here. Not just here, but around you.'

Christine's gaze dropped to the ground for a moment before she looked back up. 'I'm glad to hear that. I want you to feel comfortable.'

Hailey offered a playful smile. 'Don't worry, I'm not trying to move in permanently.'

'I didn't think you were, but just so you know, you're welcome here for as long as you need.'

'Thanks, but I can't keep depending on your generosity. I need to find something permanent. I'll start looking for a house share or something tomorrow. Anything is better than staying in a hostel.'

'Just take your time, okay? Don't rush into anything. Make sure it's the right place for you.'

'I will,' Hailey promised, a glimmer of hope starting to light up her situation.

Diary entry:

Just when I thought everything was falling apart, Christine swooped in and saved me again. And I'm sitting here, trying to wrap my head around it all. Having to leave that house and Sasha behind, it's tearing me up inside.

Lindsay's words are echoing in my head, like this constant reminder. 'It's time for things to go back to normal.' But what is normal, really? Does normal mean erasing me from their lives?

I just wish I knew where things went off track. I thought I was fitting in, finding my spot in their world.

Sasha's tears, her begging, they're all replaying in my mind. I'm making a promise to myself, like a vow. No matter what's thrown our way, I won't let us fade. I'll fight for us, even if everything's a mess right now and…

Hailey abruptly stopped writing, eyeing her words critically.

What the hell am I doing? Every time I write about things, I'm just reliving my past.

She tore the pages out of her diary. Tomorrow, she would burn them. It was time to stop living in her head.

She couldn't escape her past. It was time she stopped trying to.

Chapter Thirty-Four

With a trembling finger, Sasha pressed the doorbell, each chime echoing the rapid beats of her heart. Moments later, the door swung open, revealing Aunt Jo's warm smile that quickly faded as she took in Sasha's distressed expression.

Concern was evident in Jo's voice. 'Everything all right, sweetheart?'

'Aunt Jo, I can't do it anymore. Hailey's gone! I can't go back to that house with that woman in it, and I can't leave Chloe with her,' Sasha said, her voice teetering on the edge of tears.

'What? Gone? Gone where?'

'Mum kicked her out. She just threw her out like she was a piece of rubbish. I don't know where she's gone or what's going to happen.' Sasha's words stumbled over one another as she buried her hands in her face.

'I'm sure Hailey's fine,' Jo said calmly. 'Come on. Come inside and tell me what happened.'

Jo took hold of the pram's handle and guided it into the hallway, with Sasha following. She carefully lifted Chloe, still asleep, out of the pram and carried her through to the living room, where she gently laid her down on the sofa, cocooning her in a blanket.

'Everything was fine up until yesterday and then bam, out of the blue she tells me she wants Hailey to move out.'

'And she didn't say why?'

'That woman doesn't need a reason to be nasty. Probably woke up yesterday morning and thought of all the ways she could ruin my life.'

'Something must have set her off.'

'I don't care. All I know is that I'm not going back and I'm keeping Chloe with me. I don't care what she does anymore.'

Sitting beside Chloe, Jo spoke softly. 'Sasha, running away isn't the answer; it will only make things worse.'

Tears welled in Sasha's eyes, her vision blurring the form of her aunt before her. 'Nothing could be worse than letting Chloe grow up with my mother. I can't let her face the same pain I did. She's done nothing but made my life a misery. Well, she's won, I'm done!'

'I understand, Sasha. But you're heading down a dangerous path. Running away with Chloe isn't going to solve anything; it'll just exacerbate the situation.'

'Make it worse than it already is?' Sasha let out a bitter laugh as she paced the floor. 'Then what should I do? Stay there and endure the torment? End up like my dad, a walking, talking shell?'

'Sasha, please listen to me,' Jo implored, her voice gentle yet firm. 'I know you're hurting. But we need a plan – a thoughtful one. Impulsive actions could backfire.'

'I already have a plan,' Sasha said. 'I'm going to take Chloe to a women's refuge and tell them I'm a victim of domestic abuse, which I am. My mum might not physically hit me, but the psychological abuse is just as bad.'

'I understand,' Jo admitted, her eyes locking onto Sasha's. 'But rushing into this might not ensure Chloe's long-term safety.'

Sasha's breath caught as Aunt Jo's words resonated within her. She slumped into an armchair. 'So, what do you suggest?'

Jo looked defeated. 'I don't know, aside from getting social services involved.'

Sasha jumped to her feet, frantic. 'No way! They'll take Chloe and put her into foster care—'

'Not necessarily. I could call them and request a welfare check on Chloe. If she's on their radar, it might rattle Lindsay a bit.'

'You really think they'll believe an author whose public image revolves around helping parents is neglecting her own children? She'd probably charm them and sign copies of her book for them, knowing her.'

'That's a possibility. But that's the only option we've got. Alternatively …' Jo hesitated.

'What?'

'I could have a conversation with your dad.'

'Don't make me laugh. He doesn't care as long as he has a peaceful life; the world could go to hell.'

'It's worth a try.'

'No, it isn't. I don't trust him.'

As she voiced these words, Sasha confronted the stark reality of her life. She didn't even trust her own parents, the very people who brought her into the world and were meant to protect her.

Sasha's resolve began to waver as she stared at Chloe, her emotions tangled in a web of frustration, fear, and despair. A sense of helplessness enveloped her. She had been fighting so hard to create a better life for Chloe, to shield her from the pain she herself had endured, but now it seemed like the walls were closing in.

Jo's voice broke through her thoughts, gentle yet laden with concern. 'Sasha, I know this is overwhelming. But remember, you're not alone in this. We'll find a way through, even if it doesn't feel like it right now.'

Sasha's shoulders slumped as she realised that while the battle might feel lost in this moment, the war was far from over.

Chapter Thirty-Five

Jo's gaze lingered on the spot where Sasha had been sitting moments earlier, a tornado of emotions churning within her. As the door clicked shut, the emptiness in the room seemed to magnify. She ran a hand through her hair, her fingers trembling with a sense of helplessness.

Her heart ached for Sasha and Chloe. Jo yearned to find a way, any way at all, to lighten the heavy burden that had come to rest on her niece's fragile shoulders. Yet, with each passing day, Jo found herself grappling with the stark reality that her desire to help might inadvertently worsen the situation.

The dilemma ate away at her. She had often daydreamed about swooping in, like a guardian angel, and whisking Sasha and Chloe away from the toxicity that clung to their lives. But she knew it wasn't as simple as that. Lindsay, a formidable force of control, would never let them escape her grasp.

Jo let out a heavy sigh. She had seen Sasha's eyes, haunted by exhaustion and uncertainty, and each time she wanted to offer solutions, the fear of making things worse had silenced her.

As Jo sat lost in thought, her phone buzzed on the table. It was a message from Sasha.

Thank you for listening, Aunt Jo. It means a lot.

Jo's lips curved into a bittersweet smile. While she wished she could do more, she knew that sometimes being a listening ear was exactly what Sasha needed.

Replying with a heartfelt message, Jo hoped that her words could convey the support she felt in her heart. She wished she could articulate the depth of her desire to help, but in the absence of a clear path forward, all she could do was reaffirm her commitment to being there, no matter the challenges they faced.

Something had to give. All Jo could do is pray that when the solution came, it wasn't too late.

Chapter Thirty-Six

Sasha was in the middle of wheeling Chloe out the front door when the house phone began to ring insistently. With a sigh, she paused, gently placing Chloe's buggy by the door before reaching for the house phone and putting it to her ear.

'Hello?'

'Good morning, this is DS Matthews from Mayen Police Station. Can I speak with Sasha Miller?'

Sasha's grip on the phone tightened. 'Speaking. Is something wrong?'

Her mind raced through the possibilities. Her parents, Hailey – had they been hurt?

'No, it's nothing to worry about. I'd like to speak with you regarding the recent incidents you reported,' DS Matthews replied. 'Would you be able to come down to the police station for a talk?'

'Of course. Do you know how long you'll need me for?'

'Shouldn't be that long.'

'Okay, I'll come this afternoon on my lunch break.'

'Thank you, see you then.'

Sasha ended the call and instinctively reached for her pocket to call Hailey, only to realise her mobile phone wasn't there. Feeling the need to talk to someone, she dialled the number she knew by heart.

'Hi, Aunt Jo.'

Her tone was cautious. 'Is everything all right?'

Sasha laughed. 'That seems to be the way we all start our conversations these days.'

'Well, these are trying times.'

'Yeah, I know. I just wanted to let you know the police just called and they want me to go to the station to talk.'

'When?'

'This afternoon. I said I'd go at lunchtime.'

'In that case, I'll meet you there.'

'You don't have—'

'This is not debatable, Sasha. I'll meet you outside at one.'

'Okay, if you insist.'

Later that afternoon, Sasha found herself outside the imposing police station. As promised, Jo was waiting for her. They entered the building together and made their way to the front desk.

'I'm here to speak with DS Matthews,' Sasha stated.

The officer glanced down at her. 'Name?'

'Sasha Miller.'

After a brief exchange on the phone, the officer gestured for them to wait. They took a seat, butterflies fluttering in Sasha's stomach. DS Matthews finally appeared, greeting them both.

'Miss Miller, thank you for coming in,' he said.

Sasha introduced Jo, and they shook hands.

He led them down a series of corridors to a small

office. As they entered, Sasha's nerves intensified. Another police officer was already present. She introduced herself as DSI Carter.

'Miss Miller—'

'Just call me Sasha.'

DSI Carter smiled. 'Sure, Sasha. We have compiled a set of photos of individuals with prior records,' Detective Carter explained. 'We're hoping you can identify the person who was stalking you.'

'I'll try.' Sasha sat down at the table and Jo stood close behind.

As the photographs were spread out in front of her, Sasha's heart pounded in her chest. She scanned the faces, her eyes narrowing as they fell upon one particular image. The familiarity of the features struck her, and she felt a pang of recognition.

DSI Carter leaned forward. 'Do any of these individuals look familiar to you?'

Sasha hesitated, her fingers trembling as she pointed at the photograph that had caught her attention. 'I … I think it might be him.'

DSI Carter exchanged a glance with DS Matthews.

'From the description you gave us, we thought it might have been him, but after speaking to him, he has a solid alibi.'

'What does that mean?'

'It means, unless we find evidence to the contrary, it's unlikely it's him.'

Wondering why Aunt Jo hadn't spoken yet, Sasha finally tore her gaze away from the pictures and turned to her. But what she saw made her gasp in shock. Aunt Jo's face had turned an ashen white, her usually warm complexion drained of all colour.

'Aunt Jo!?' Sasha's voice trembled with concern. 'Are you okay?'

Jo's lips quivered as if she wanted to say something, but no words came out.

Her eyes were fixed on one particular photograph, her expression a mixture of shock, fear, and disbelief.

Sasha followed Aunt Jo's gaze and looked at the photograph that had affected her so strongly. It was the picture of the man Sasha thought she recognised.

'What is it, Aunt Jo?' Sasha asked again, her own anxiety growing.

Aunt Jo pointed a shaky finger at the picture, her voice was barely a whisper when she finally spoke. 'It can't be.'

Chapter Thirty-Seven

Jo walked out of the police station, her steps unsteady, her usually confident demeanour shaken to its core. Sasha walked alongside her, her concern evident as she glanced at Jo.

'You looked like you recognised him.'

Jo's lips trembled as if she wanted to say something, but no words came out. Sasha gently touched her arm, offering support.

'Come on,' Sasha said softly, guiding Jo towards a nearby bar. 'Let's sit down and talk.'

They stepped into the bar, Sasha taking the lead as she guided Jo towards an available table. Jo settled onto a well-worn leather seat. Meanwhile, Sasha made her way to the bar counter.

I can't believe this, I just can't.

Moments later, Sasha placed a glass of brandy in front of her and Jo's hands trembled as she brought the glass to her lips, taking a long sip. She set the glass down, her gaze fixed on the amber liquid.

Sasha watched her closely, her concern deepening. 'Aunt Jo, you're really shaken. What did you see back there?'

She took a deep breath, gathering her thoughts before finally finding the words to speak.

'The man in the hoodie, Sasha ... he's your dad's son,' Jo said before taking another sip of her drink.

'What're you talking about? My dad hasn't got any other kids. There's just me and Chloe.'

'I'm sorry, Sasha. Miles is your half-brother.'

'I don't understand what you're saying,' Sasha said, shaking her head. 'If my dad had another kid, he would've said something.'

'I suppose he just wanted to put the past behind him as far as he could, or should I say, Lindsay did.'

'What's my mum got to do with it?'

Jo's lips quivered as she fought back tears. 'Miles is the son that Josh gave up for adoption after his mother died. Lindsay made him choose between keeping his son or keeping her. And he chose her.'

Sasha's shock was evident, her gaze shifting between Jo and her glass. 'What! I can't get my head around this. What a bitch! What a fucking bitch. And my dad, what a fucking waste of space.'

Jo reached over and placed her hand overs Sasha's. 'I understand you're angry—'

'Angry? That's an understatement.' Tears rolled down her cheeks. 'I fucking hate them both.'

She stared at Jo. 'If you knew, why didn't you tell me?'

'I wanted to, believe me. Too many times to remember, but Lindsay said if I ever told you, I'd never see you again.' Jo's shoulders slumped, her expression heavy with regret. 'I'd already lost one nephew; I couldn't risk losing you too.'

'So why didn't you fight for him?'

'I tried, Sasha. I fought for custody until it nearly

bankrupted me. But Lindsay … she spread awful lies about me, twisted the truth until the court awarded custody to another family.'

Sasha sighed. 'Why doesn't that surprise me.'

'Lindsay has shown time and time again that she's willing to go to extreme lengths to control the situation. If you confront her now about Miles, she might isolate you from Chloe, or even worse, if she thinks the truth will come out.'

'So, what do you suggest we do? Try and track him down?'

'No. Wait for him to come to you.'

'What if he doesn't?'

'He will.'

Chapter Thirty-Eight

Hailey's phone buzzed on the bedside cabinet, a sound that sent a rush of anticipation through her veins. With a quick, hopeful smile, she picked up her phone, expecting to see a message from Sasha, but as her eyes scanned the notification, her expression shifted from excitement to disbelief. Her heart plummeted as she read the words on the screen.

It wasn't a message from Sasha.

Instead, it was an email from her workplace, the subject line heavy with ominous implications.

Hailey tapped on the email and the message unfolded before her, the words like a harsh slap to her face. She felt her stomach churn as she read the content.

Dear Hailey,

We regret to inform you that your employment with us is terminated. After reviewing recent developments, we have determined that your values and actions do not align with the company's principles. We wish you all the best in your future endeavours.

Yours sincerely

Marcus Bloom

Hailey's mind raced as she tried to process the message. Fired? Values not aligned?

What the fuck is he talking about?

She had worked tirelessly, pouring dedication into her job, and now she was being let go without any explanation. The room around her seemed to blur as her shock turned into anger, her phone slipping from her fingers and onto the bed.

Quickly, she dialled Marcus's number, urgency pushing her fingers to navigate the touchscreen. The phone rang, each tone echoing like a heartbeat in her ears. Finally, he answered.

'Hi, Marcus, it's Hailey,' she spoke into the phone, her tone full of both curiosity and concern. 'I just got your email. Am I missing something?'

There was a brief pause on the other end before Marcus responded, his voice guarded. 'Hailey, I don't have much time to talk right now.'

Hailey's pulse quickened, her grip on the phone tightening.

'But I don't understand. I thought you were happy with my work.'

'I was, but I need people on my team that I can trust.'

Confusion crept into Hailey's words. 'What? Did something happen?'

'A serious accusation has been made, and as you're only on probation, we've decided to terminate your employment.' Marcus let out a sigh.

Hailey's heart pounded, her mind racing to piece

together the puzzle. 'What are you talking about?'

'I've said enough. Goodbye, Hailey.' Marcus's tone was final, and the line went dead, leaving Hailey staring at her phone in disbelief.

Lindsay's got to be behind this!

'What the fuck did Lindsay tell him?' The words slipped from her lips in a hushed whisper, her mind whirling.

The name flashed in her mind like a neon sign, a glaring accusation that seemed to fit perfectly with the circumstances. She couldn't let Lindsay get away with sabotaging her like this. She couldn't allow herself to be a pawn in whatever twisted game Lindsay seemed to be playing.

Despite her unease, Hailey knew she had to face this head-on – she couldn't let Lindsay's actions go unchecked. With a determined expression, she grabbed her bag and headed to the bus stop. Twenty minutes later, she stepped off the bus and made her way purposefully to confront Lindsay. The knot of tension in her stomach grew as she reached the front door.

Hailey's knuckles rapped sharply against the wood. Moments later, the door swung open, revealing Lindsay's figure framed by the doorway. Hailey's anger flared at the sight of her, the calmness in Lindsay's expression only fuelling her frustration.

'What do you want, Hailey?' Lindsay's voice held a mocking edge, her gaze cold and calculating.

Hailey's fists clenched at her sides, her nails digging into her palms. She fought to keep her voice steady, despite the anger raging within her.

'What did you do?' Her words quivered with restrained emotion. 'Did you think ruining my job would somehow break me? Is that your sick idea of revenge?'

Lindsay's lips curled into a self-satisfied smirk, infuriating Hailey even more.

'You give yourself way more importance than you deserve.'

The words stung, and Hailey's anger intensified.

'You think you can control everyone's lives, don't you? Well, newsflash, Lindsay: you can't.'

Lindsay's eyes sparked with malice, and she stepped closer, invading Hailey's personal space.

'Hailey, you really don't want to cross me, believe me. I can make your life hell if you overstep the mark again. Get that heap of junk off my driveway. Stay away from this house and stay away from Sasha and you—'

'What? What more can you do? And you can't keep me away from Sasha.'

A cruel smile twisted Lindsay's lip. 'Oh, a lot more. Do you really think anyone would hesitate to believe me if I told them … oh, I dunno, that you stole from me? That you took my precious jewellery that belonged to my dear nanna?'

A chill ran down Hailey's spine at the threat in Lindsay's words. Her anger was momentarily replaced by a growing fear.

'You wouldn't.'

'Try me.'

'You're one sick person, d'you know that? You might have people fooled now, but they'll see your true colours one day.'

Lindsay's smile faded, replaced by a cold, calculating expression. 'I doubt it, but dream on if it makes you feel better.'

'We'll see about that, won't we?'

As Hailey turned to leave, Lindsay's threat lingered ominously in the air. Hailey couldn't shake the feeling that Lindsay's manipulation was just beginning.

Chapter Thirty-Nine

Walking out of the university doors, Sasha's head was still spinning from the bombshell about her half-brother, a person she had no idea even existed. It was like someone had rewritten her life's script overnight, and she was left trying to make sense of the new plot twists. Anger, confusion, and hurt simmered within her as she grappled with the fact that her parents had kept such a huge secret from her.

Hearing her name being called, she turned and spotted Hailey. There was an automatic smile on her lips as she rushed into her waiting arms.

'Hey,' Hailey whispered.

'Oh my god, I've missed you,' Sasha said, squeezing Hailey tightly.

'I've missed you too,' Hailey replied, a hint of sadness in her voice. As they pulled back slightly, their eyes met, and Sasha couldn't help but let out a small sigh.

'You've not been reading my messages,' Hailey said.

'My mum took my phone off me.'

'I'm surprised she has so much time on her hands, seeing as she's trying to ruin my life,' Hailey continued, her frustration evident.

'What d'you mean?'

'She got me fired.'

'What!?'

Hailey nodded, bitterness in her voice. 'They came out with some rubbish about their values not aligning with mine. Someone had made an accusation against me. I think we both know who that was.'

'I thought I knew her, but I really don't. Hailey … I … I know who the guy wearing the hoodie is.'

An alarmed expression crossed Hailey's face. 'He didn't—'

'He doesn't want to hurt me …'

'How'd you know?'

'Because he's my brother. Well, my half-brother.'

'Your what? Please tell me you're joking.'

'I wish I were.'

They continued to walk, heading towards an open green space.

'Wait, how did you find out?' Hailey asked.

Seating themselves on a bench, Sasha took a deep breath. 'Aunt Jo told me.'

Hailey's eyebrows shot up. 'She's known this whole time? Wow, she could be a professional spy – nothing seems to faze her.'

Sasha managed a rueful smile. 'Yeah, seems like keeping secrets runs in the family.'

Sasha slid her arm around Hailey's waist and rested her head on her shoulder. 'Families are so messed up.'

'Tell me about it,' Hailey said, kissing her on the top of her head. 'So, do you want to meet him?'

'I dunno. I'm still trying to wrap my head around it and what it means.'

'Yeah, I get where you're coming from. It must've been a massive shock.'

'It was.'

There was a brief silence as they both contemplated the situation.

'So, what about you? Where did Christine take you?'

'To her house.'

'Really?'

'Yep, she said I could stay as long as I want.'

'D'you think she'd let me come over?'

'I don't see why not, but maybe in a few days. I don't want to seem like I'm taking the piss.'

'Well, Jo said we can meet round her place if we want to,' Sasha said, looking up at Hailey.

'Your aunt's so cool, and I think we should.'

'I'll let her know.'

Hailey got to her feet. 'Come on.'

'Where're we going?'

'To buy you a phone. If your mum thinks she's going to keep us apart, she's more delusional than I thought she was.'

As she was about to start walking, Sasha spotted Miles, hood still pulled over his head, his body angled in her direction. Her heart raced, but this time, instead of succumbing to fear, she felt a surge of adrenaline. Without hesitating, Sasha walked purposefully towards him. As she neared, his eyes widened slightly with surprise, and he began to back away.

Sasha quickened her pace, her determination fuelling her steps.

'Hey, Miles, I know who you are!' she called out, her voice strong and unwavering. 'Wait!'

Miles picked up his pace, but Sasha was relentless. She broke into a run, her heart pounding in her chest. Her breath echoed in her ears as she closed the distance between them.

With a burst of energy, Sasha managed to catch up to Miles, her fingers gripping his shoulder firmly. He turned around, his hood falling back to reveal his face. Her lips parted. Miles was the spitting image of her dad.

'Aunt Jo told me about you. Do you remember her?'

Miles took a step towards her and opened his mouth as if about to speak, but before he could utter a word, a voice behind her cut through the air.

'Sasha!'

'I'm … s-sorry about the window. I-I didn't mean to scare you.'

Sasha turned to see Hailey approaching. Miles saw his chance and acted on it, forcefully manoeuvring past Sasha and launching into a sprint. In a matter of seconds, he disappeared into the dense cover of the surrounding trees.

'No! Fuck!' Sasha shouted, but it was too late. He had vanished, leaving her standing there, frustration and disappointment flooding her.

Hailey reached her, breath slightly laboured.

'Are you okay?'

'Yeah.'

Hailey tried to catch her breath. 'Who was that?'

'My brother.'

'When you took off like that, I didn't know where you were going. I understand you wanted to talk to him, but you have to be careful. Confronting him like that could've been dangerous. You don't know anything about him.'

'I know, and you're right.'

Gazing towards the spot where Miles had disappeared, Sasha couldn't help but wonder if she would ever see him again.

And more importantly: Did she want to?

Chapter Forty

'This feels like a secret hook-up,' Hailey said, pressing Sasha against the wall in Jo's hallway before covering her mouth with her own.

'It adds to the excitement,' Sasha said.

Their lips met again in a heated kiss, the intensity of their connection igniting a fire within them. Sasha's fingers tangled in Hailey's hair, their bodies pressing closer, as if trying to make up for lost time.

'How long do we have until your aunt gets home?' Hailey said between kisses, her words a husky whisper against Sasha's lips.

Sasha pulled away slightly, their heavy breaths mingling in the air. 'Not long enough to do what you want.'

Hailey let out a playful laugh. 'You're no fun.'

'Oh, I'm plenty of fun,' Sasha replied with a playful smirk, her fingers tracing a tantalizing pattern on Hailey's back.

'So, what's with all the urgency? Have you changed your mind about running away with me?'

Sasha's gaze turned serious, her eyes locking with Hailey's.

'I wish I could.'

Hailey's fingers brushed a strand of hair away from Sasha's face, her touch gentle. 'What's your mother been up to now?'

Sasha's lips pressed into a thin line as she looked away, her expression troubled.

'Well … I thought she was just bluffing, but after finding out about my brother, I know she'd really do it.'

Hailey's grip instinctively tightened around Sasha's hand. 'Do what?'

'Put Chloe up for adoption.'

'Fuck! Is that what she's been telling you to keep you in line?'

Sasha nodded. 'She's been holding it over my head from the day Chloe was born.'

Hailey took a step back, her frustration and anger evident. She tilted her head to the ceiling, as if seeking solace from the world.

'Fucking hell. That woman is pure evil.'

'I know,' Sasha said softly, her voice filled with resignation. 'And that's why … I'm going to have to do what she says … We'll have to be extra careful and not see each other as much.'

The hallway seemed to close in around them, the confines of their situation becoming suffocating.

'This is so unfair!' Hailey said.

Sasha nodded, her lips trembling as she fought to hold back tears. 'I know, but I can't let anything happen to Chloe. I'd never forgive myself.'

Hailey walked down the hallway and sat on the stairs, her frustration and helplessness evident. 'So we're fucked either way. Chloe will end up in a home, and I'll end up in prison.'

Sasha's brow furrowed. 'What are you on about?'

Hailey let out a bitter laugh. 'You had enough to deal with, so I wasn't going to tell you. Your mum said she'd tell the police I stole her jewellery if I didn't stay away from you.'

Sasha's eyes widened. 'She said what?'

'Don't look surprised. This is your mother we're talking about.'

Sasha joined Hailey on the stairs. 'I'm so sorry you got caught up in all this mess.'

Hailey nudged her playfully, her attempt at lightening the mood. 'It's worth it. I'd never have met you otherwise.'

The doorbell rang and they exchanged a curious glance.

'Did your aunt forget her keys?' Hailey said.

'I dunno.'

The doorbell rang again.

'Whoever it is, they're persistent,' Sasha said as she reluctantly rose to her feet and approached the door. Pulling it back, the sight that greeted her froze her in her tracks.

'Dad, what're you doing here?'

'I could ask you the same. Why aren't you at university?'

Sasha's response was quick, a hint of defensiveness in her tone. 'I have free periods this afternoon.'

'Does your mum know?'

Sasha shook her head.

Josh's gaze shifted, his attention drawn to Hailey

who had walked up behind Sasha. 'If your mum finds out about this, there'll be hell to pay.'

'I know,' Sasha said.

He let out a long sigh. 'Is Jo in?'

'No, but she shouldn't be too long.'

'In that case, I'll wait.'

Josh's entrance marked the beginning of an uneasy silence, the three of them walking into the kitchen, the tension palpable. They settled at the table, their thoughts and emotions speaking volumes in the quiet.

A few moments later, the sharp sound of the door slamming shut drew their attention.

Jo walked in, her surprise evident when she saw Josh sitting at the table. 'What do I owe the pleasure?' she asked, placing her shopping bags on the table.

'Can we talk … alone?' Josh asked.

Jo's gaze shifted to Sasha, who gave a slight shrug. 'I've got to get back to uni anyway. Let's go, Hailey.'

Once outside, they remained standing on the pathway, looking back at the house.

'I'd love to be a fly on the wall to hear what they're talking about,' Hailey said.

'Me too.'

As if on cue, Hailey's phone beeped with a notification. She retrieved it from her pocket and stared down at it.

'What're you looking like that for? Has someone sent you a dick pic?' Sasha teased.

Hailey's gaze remained focused on her phone,

her expression serious as she slowly shook her head.

'It's from your mum. She knows I'm with you, Sash … but that's not the worst part. She knows exactly where we are.'

Chapter Forty-One

Lindsay reviewed the newly written chapter with a contented sigh, leaning back in her chair, thoroughly satisfied. The story had exceeded her wildest expectations. She had realised from the moment she met Christine, that their paths were destined to cross. Bringing Hailey into their home had proven to be a pivotal decision, rescuing her floundering writing career. Now, fuelled by Hailey's tumultuous experiences, she was poised to reclaim her position at the top.

Lindsay shifted her attention to the next chapter, seeking a spark of inspiration. As she opened a new page, her fingers instinctively reached for the stack of photocopied papers in the drawer.

What the …

A sense of unease washed over her. She looked from the computer to the drawer, her heart quickening as realisation struck: the diary was missing.

Panic surged, its grip tightening around her like a vice.

Abruptly standing, her office turned chaotic, drawers open, papers scattered. Minutes passed, frustration building. Just as desperation loomed, the office door opened.

'Lindsay, what's going on?' Josh said, looking around the office with raised eyebrows.

'Sasha's been in my office. She's taken something

of mine.'

'Are you sure you haven't misplaced it?'

Her rage burned.

'Where! Look at this place. Don't you think I would've found it by now?'

Josh's calm voice countered, 'Let's not jump to conclusions. Sasha knows not to mess with your stuff. Whatever it is you've lost, I'm sure we can find it.'

'It's. Not. Fucking. Here. Are you stupid!'

Josh remained calm. 'Lindsay, take a breath. Reacting impulsively won't serve anyone well. Let's have a word with her and see what she has to say.'

'What she has to say? She'll fucking lie, like she always does.'

No, she wouldn't simply confront Sasha; she would make her pay, make her understand the gravity of her actions. Lindsay's fingers curled into tight fists, her nails biting into her palms as a storm of thoughts raged within her.

'We'll get it back. Now, why don't you pour yourself a drink and I'll tidy up this mess.'

His words were a balm to her seething emotions, a reminder that a measured approach was more effective than a blind rush. Lindsay's shoulders tensed as she forced herself to relax, her hands slowly unclenching.

I'm going to make her wish she was never born!

Chapter Forty-Two

Sasha found herself alone on a weathered bench, the world around her a distant backdrop. This moment of solitude was a reprieve from the storm that had enveloped her life.

Recent weeks had turned her reality upside down. The revelation of a half-brother's existence had been a seismic shock, leaving her grappling with a new identity. But that was only the beginning. Falling in love with Hailey had painted the world with vibrant colours, until her mother's calculated interference cast a shadow over it all. And now, in the midst of this chaos, her father's unexpected appearance at her aunt's home.

What the hell is going on? And how did her mother know where Hailey was?

The only explanation she could come up with was that her dad had told her mother.

But the more she thought about it, the more she realised it didn't make sense. Aunt Jo and her dad had been estranged for years, likely due to her mother's controlling nature, so she couldn't imagine him letting her mother know he was at her aunt's house.

How else could she have ... A realisation struck her with an icy jolt: the new phone her mother had gifted Hailey. She must have put a tracking app on it. The notion that her mother could do such a thing didn't surprise her. But why? Why was her mother so invested in Hailey's every move? What twisted motive could be behind it?

She thought back to the papers she had glimpsed in her mother's office. What were they, exactly? They had appeared to be some sort of record, like a diary of sorts. Could the answers she sought be hidden within those pages? There was only one way to find out: wait until her mother was asleep and venture into the office once again.

With a reluctant sigh, Sasha pushed herself up from the bench and began her journey back to the university.

As she walked the corridors towards her first lecture, a voice called out her name.

'Sasha, can I have a word?' Dr Anderson's voice stopped her in her tracks.

'Um, sure,' Sasha responded, the question prompting her to change her course and approach her tutor's office. She entered and Dr Anderson motioned for Sasha to take a seat opposite her desk.

Sitting down, Sasha's mind raced. 'Have I done something wrong?'

Dr Anderson's smile was warm, though tinged with concern. 'Of course not. I just wanted to see how things are with you.'

'Oh, right.'

'Is everything okay at home?' Dr Anderson's question took Sasha by surprise.

'Um, yeah, I s'pose. Why?' Sasha tried to keep her tone casual, though a sense of unease crept in.

'I don't mean to pry, and please feel free to tell me to back off, but I'm worried about you,' Dr Anderson explained gently. 'You've been skipping lectures and your coursework has been late, or not turned in at all.'

Sasha shifted uncomfortably in her seat, the truth of Dr Anderson's words hitting her with a pang of guilt. 'I'm sorry, but things have been hectic recently.'

Dr Anderson leaned forward, her expression compassionate. 'Is there anything I can do to help? If there's something going on, I want you to know that you can talk to me.'

The genuine concern in her eyes was both touching and overwhelming. Sasha felt her throat tighten and she blinked back tears.

She shook her head, her voice barely above a whisper. 'No, thank you. I appreciate it, but it's something I have to figure out myself.'

Dr Anderson nodded, her gaze steady. 'All right, just remember that I'm here if you need me.'

Sasha managed a small smile, before standing and leaving her office. Her mother's actions were casting a shadow over every aspect of her life. If Sasha couldn't find a way to untangle the mess, an uncertain and daunting future awaited her.

Chapter Forty-Three

Hailey's mind was a mess. Nothing made sense anymore. How had things spiralled out of control so quickly? The promising new life she had envisioned on the horizon had faded away as swiftly as a gorgeous sunset. And it wasn't just her own life; Sasha's had been ensnared in this turmoil too. Hailey's trust had been misplaced, her faith in Lindsay a bitter pill to swallow. She berated herself for falling for the façade, for believing in the kindness that was nothing more than an illusion. Revealing the truth to Christine wasn't an option, as she would only blame herself for entrusting Hailey into the care of a pathological liar.

Hailey had met a fair share of dodgy people in her life, but the only thing that separated them from Lindsay was that they showed their true colours upfront. Lindsay was a master of deception, which was way more dangerous.

It still shocked her that Lindsay had forced Josh into a choice between her and his son, and he had ultimately picked Lindsay. She could only attribute such a cowardly action to Josh being engulfed by grief over the loss of his former wife. What other explanation could there be? From what she had seen of Josh, he didn't strike her as a callous man, but then again what did she know? She had mistakenly thought Lindsay was a beacon of light.

The upstairs door slammed shut, and Hailey wondered why Christine had returned early from work. Then, it struck her that Christine had mentioned her husband Robert returning today from a business trip. Footsteps echoed through the hallway, then down the stairs, drawing closer to her room.

The door slowly creaked open, and a tall figure stood in the doorway. His presence was overwhelming, his eyes fixed on her as if he were seeing a ghost. The awkward silence stretched between them, laden with unspoken tension.

'Hi,' Hailey managed, her voice a bit too high-pitched, betraying her discomfort.

He nodded, his expression inscrutable. Hadn't Christine informed him about her stay? The weight of his gaze bore into her, making her squirm under its intensity. Hailey wasn't one to shy away from awkwardness, but this was different.

'I was just about to head out,' Hailey said, her words hurried. 'I just need to grab a few things.'

As he remained silent, Hailey's discomfort grew. She realised she was trapped in the basement with him blocking her way out. Panic surged. Would he allow her to leave or hold her captive in this room?

Hailey tried to calm her mind, telling herself that she was imagining things, but something was amiss by the way he kept staring at her wordlessly. Her instincts told her to at least try to leave by any means possible. Or at least get off the bed. If she was standing, she'd have half a chance of kicking him between his legs to give her more time to escape.

She took out her phone and kept it tightly in her hand with every intention of calling the police if he made one false move.

Hailey slung her bag over her shoulder and got to her feet.

'It was nice to meet you. Robert, right?' Her words were cautious as she approached him slowly, her movements calculated.

'I … eh …' he stammered.

'Okay, so can you tell Christine I'll be back later tonight?'

'Yes.'

Suddenly, he stepped aside, granting her passage as if coming to his senses. His unbroken gaze tracked her as she hurried to the stairs. Fear pushed her forward, propelling her up the steps as fast as she could manage. Once outside, she sprinted down the road putting as much distance as she could between her and the house.

The cool breeze offered a momentary respite from the anxiety that had gripped her. She finally came to a stop and leaned against the edge of a bench, taking deep breaths to steady herself. It was in that moment that she made a decision. She couldn't go back there. She was not going to put herself in a vulnerable position again for anyone. Not even Christine. She couldn't help but wonder if Christine knew she was married to a creepy pervert.

Hailey dialled the number of the hostel Christine had taken her to before.

She spoke to the manager, explaining her situation and was told her room was still available. Moving to the hostel would mean leaving behind the comfort she had found at Christine's, but so be it. She'd rather take her chances at the hostel. Anything was preferable to being trapped in a basement, where a man with questionable intentions roamed freely in the night.

Chapter Forty-Four

Lindsay stood at the entrance of the house, her eyes ablaze with anger as Sasha made her way up the path.

'Sasha!' She practically spat the name, her voice sharp and accusatory. 'Where are they?'

Sasha blinked rapidly. 'Where are what?'

Relief flooded her. This wasn't about her being with Hailey. At least that gave her time to think up an explanation as for why they were at her aunt's house together.

Lindsay's face contorted with rage as Sasha passed her and walked down the hallway. 'Don't play dumb with me! You know exactly what I'm talking about. The papers in my desk drawer! Why did you take them?'

Sasha's mind raced, confused. She had no idea what her mother was talking about. She had left them exactly where they were. 'I swear, Mum, I didn't take anything from your office.'

Lindsay's eyes narrowed dangerously, her voice a seething hiss. 'Don't lie to me! I know you've been snooping around in my personal belongings.'

Josh looked up when she entered the living room, Lindsay at her heel.

'Lindsay, I thought we decided to talk about this in a rational manner.'

His words fell on deaf ears as Lindsay's fury

intensified.

'Stay out of this, Josh!' Lindsay snapped, her attention squarely on Sasha. 'I want those papers back, and I want them now!'

Sasha's voice raised in response to her mother's anger. 'I'm telling you, I don't have any papers! I don't know why you're accusing me of doing something I didn't do!'

Lindsay's nostrils flared as she continued to berate Sasha. 'You're just like your father, always trying to undermine me, always trying to ruin everything!'

'Me ruin things? That's rich coming from you. That's all you ever do, you can't help yourself, can you? It's like second nature to you, spreading your misery and hate—'

Lindsay lunged forward, her face mere inches from Sasha's. 'How dare you talk to me like that! You're going to regret—'

'The only thing I regret is not fucking standing up to you before now. I hate you!'

Without another word, Sasha brushed past Lindsay and fled, running to her room and slamming the door behind her.

She started to think that perhaps her aunt had been right about involving social services. Her mother was unhinged, and it was only a matter of time before her behaviour worsened.

Suddenly, the sound of a stone hitting her window shattered the tense silence that had enveloped her room. She rushed to the window thinking it was Hailey and peered out, her eyes widening. It was Miles. He stood across the road, his face obscured by the darkness of his hoodie, beckoning her to come outside.

Should she go? The rational portion of her thoughts cried out for caution, urging her to consider the danger of meeting someone who, despite sharing blood, remained essentially a stranger. But another part of her, the part that craved answers and closure, was tempted to take the risk.

Sasha's fingers trembled as she hastily pulled out her phone and typed a message to Hailey. The glow of the screen illuminated her face as she sent a quick text, desperately seeking guidance.

Miles is outside. He wants me to go down. What should I do?

Seconds ticked by as she waited for Hailey's reply.
Finally, a notification chimed, and Sasha quickly read Hailey's response.

Do NOT go outside! Stay where you are!

Her eyes darted back out the window where Miles was still stood, waiting.

She clutched her phone tightly, fingers trembling as she struggled to make a decision.

In the end, her heart won over her curiosity. With a heavy sigh, she turned away from the window and took a step back. She replied to Hailey's text.

All right. I won't go. But I can't help feeling bad for him.

I get it, Sasha. Just remember, you don't know anything about him.

I know, you're right! Ok, my mum's at it again with her nonsense, so I'm gonna hide my phone in case she comes up. Speak later.

She was just about to type 'love you' when she suddenly stopped, the revelation surprising her. *I do love her.*

But now wasn't the time to make her feelings known over a text message. She'd wait until she saw Hailey in person so she could gauge how she felt too. She signed off with 'xx' instead and switched off the phone before hiding it at the bottom of her wardrobe.

A stone sounded against her window again.

Urgh! He isn't going to go away if I don't talk to him. Sorry, Hailey, but I've got to trust my gut instinct.

Sasha carefully unlatched the window, the cool caress of night air brushing against her face as she stepped onto the windowsill and descended the drainpipe to the soft embrace of grass below. Miles stood a short distance away, a mysterious figure against the dark backdrop. As Sasha approached him, her anxiety intensified when he gestured for her to follow.

She trailed behind him through the silent night,

the only sound punctuating the stillness being the hushed crunch of leaves underfoot. The passage of time seemed to stretch as Miles led her to a small clearing nestled amidst the trees.

Her voice trembled, breaking the quiet as she spoke. 'What's going on?'

'I just ... I wanted to meet you.'

'Why follow me? Break the window? I don't understand.'

'I didn't know how to approach you, or if you'd even believe me. Then, that day, I saw Lindsay in the window and saw red. I'm sorry.'

'But the police said you had an alibi.'

He smirked. 'I have some good friends.'

'Do you remember Aunt Jo?'

His nod was a subtle acknowledgment of the past they shared.

The weight of guilt pressed on Sasha's chest, and she felt the need to apologise. 'I'm so sorry, Miles. I didn't know anything about you until Aunt Jo told me what happened. I can't believe what my mum did ...'

'My dad had a choice,' he interjected.

'I know.' Sasha's voice held empathy. 'They're just as bad as each other.'

Questions swirled in Sasha's mind, each fighting for her attention, yet she was uncertain where to start. 'How did you find us?'

Miles's reply was straightforward, devoid of hesitation. 'It was easy. I found Lindsay online and followed her home from a book reading.'

Sasha raked her fingers through her hair. 'Have you spoken to Dad? Has he seen you?'

'No. I'm not ready yet,' he confessed.

'Ready for what?'

'To confront him. He's probably forgotten all about me.'

'I doubt it, Miles,' Sasha said. 'How could he? You're his son. My big brother.'

For a brief moment, a fleeting smile softened his face.

'Can we—'

Before she could complete her sentence, the sound of approaching footsteps neared.

'Where can I find you?' she asked, desperation evident in her tone.

Miles's attention shifted beyond her, his gaze narrowing on something unseen behind her.

He turned to go, his movement swift and decisive. But before he could escape into the shadows, Sasha's desperation gave way to determination. She lunged forward, her fingers curling around his arm as she stopped him in his tracks.

'Go and see Aunt Jo, Miles. Please,' she said, quickly telling him Jo's address.

He shrugged off her grip, his eyes a storm of conflicting emotions. Suddenly, he turned and sprinted into the night, leaving Sasha standing alone in the clearing.

Finally, the approaching footsteps reached her, and she turned to face her neighbour, walking his dog.

As he passed by with a nod of greeting, Sasha's shoulders slumped, and she let out a long sigh as she started her journey home.

All she could do now was pray that Miles would heed her plea and reach out to Aunt Jo, perhaps rekindling a connection long overdue.

***

Sasha had successfully managed to evade her mother's presence throughout the entire night, even skipping dinner to avoid any potential confrontation. She didn't trust herself to hold her tongue, knowing that speaking her mind would only escalate matters further. Unable to find solace in sleep, she quietly slipped into Hailey's old room, a space that had transformed into a refuge for both of them. The walls seemed to resonate with the echoes of their late-night talks, shared laughter, and the profound comfort they found in each other's companionship.

With a heavy sigh, Sasha stretched out on the bed, wrapping her arms around a pillow and clutching it close. It was as if she hoped to capture a fragment of the warmth and connection she had shared with Hailey. The room, once a haven, now felt incomplete without her.

Lost in her thoughts, Sasha jumped when the door creaked open. Lindsay's figure appeared in the doorway, disdain evident in her expression.

'What are you doing in here?' Lindsay's voice dripped with contempt, as though Sasha's mere presence was an offence.

Quickly brushing away a stray tear, Sasha responded, 'I was just … Nothing.'

Lindsay's gaze sharpened as she moved deeper into the room, her critical eyes scanning every corner. 'I need to get this place redecorated, wipe away every trace of that girl's existence.'

A wave of melancholy washed over Sasha – not just for herself and Hailey, but even for her mother. She pitied Lindsay, recognising her as a bitter and callous person who had never truly known the depth of love or the art of letting someone in.

Shaking her head slightly, Sasha said, 'What did Dad see in you, Mum? What made him sacrifice his life to be with someone so bitter and twisted?'

Lindsay's composed demeanour faltered, taken aback by her words.

Sasha rose to her feet, stepping closer to her mother until they were face to face.

'D'you know what? I think Chloe would be better off in care. At least there, she'd stand a chance of being nurtured by someone capable of real love. Because you …' Sasha's voice held a hint of sorrow. 'You're not capable of loving even yourself, let alone anyone else.'

With that, Sasha left the room, a sense of liberation engulfing her. She felt unburdened, finally free from the toxic ties that bound her to the woman who had brought her into the world.

Chapter Forty-Five

Christine opened the door and frowned upon seeing Hailey. 'I thought you were coming back last night.'

Hailey shuffled uncomfortably on her feet. 'Sorry, I was at a party and it finished late. I didn't want to disturb you.'

'You could have texted me and let me know. I was worried when you didn't answer your phone.'

'Sorry,' Hailey said, her gaze falling to the ground. She hated lying to Christine, but she couldn't tell her the truth.

'Have you eaten? Can I—'

'I'm good, thanks,' Hailey interjected, a tired smile attempting to soften the awkwardness of the situation.

'Hailey, something seems off. What's bothering you?'

That was the problem with Christine, she could read her like a book.

Hailey's shoulders slumped as she walked a few steps down the hallway. 'Um, nothing … Look, Christine, I've actually decided to move into the hostel.'

Christine's surprise was evident in the way her brows shot up. 'What? Why?'

Hailey brushed past her, making her way down

to her room. Christine followed closely, while Hailey began the task of gathering her scattered belongings.

'I just need my own space for a while, you know? Time to figure things out on my own. I appreciate your offer to let me stay here, but I need to stand on my own two feet. It's time to stop leaning on you so much.'

Christine's eyes dimmed slightly, sadness in her expression. 'Being a part of your life has been very special to me.'

'And that won't change. I just need to find my own way without constantly relying on you. You can't be my safety net forever.'

Christine's voice softened. 'Yes, I can, and for as long as you need.'

Hailey shook her head, her resolve hardening. 'That's the problem. At this rate, I'll never truly learn to handle things myself.' With a sense of finality, she zipped up her suitcase. 'Can you help me with my things, please?'

She wanted to get out of there as fast as she could. She'd been hiding across the street all morning, waiting for Robert to leave so she could collect her stuff without running the risk of bumping into him again.

As they lugged the suitcase upstairs and reached the front door, Christine held onto Hailey's shoulders.

'Keep me posted on how you're settling in, okay?'

'I will. We can meet for coffee during the week if you're free.'

'I'd like that.'

'Okay, see you soon,' Hailey said, setting off down the path.

She made a conscious effort not to look back. The prospect of witnessing the sadness etched on Christine's face was something Hailey had to avoid, understanding that the sight would only make the act of leaving even more difficult.

Arriving back at her hostel, she unpacked and made the best of the small place as she could, cleaning it within an inch of its life. It wasn't great, but it was her home for the foreseeable future.

A smile spread across her face as her phone rang, the caller ID revealing Sasha's name.

'Hey, you busy?' Sasha asked.

'Never too busy for you.'

'I'm at the park with Chloe. Wanna come and hang out?'

'I'll be there before you know it,' Hailey said, already slipping into her jacket.

Hailey's steps quickened as she entered the park, her gaze scanning the familiar surroundings until she spotted Sasha by the pond, Chloe's buggy parked beside her.

'Sasha!' Hailey called out.

Sasha turned towards the sound of her name, her eyes lighting up as she saw Hailey approaching. The distance between them seemed to vanish as they closed in for a heartfelt embrace.

'I didn't know it was possible to miss someone so much,' Sasha said.

Hailey managed a small laugh. 'Me neither.'

As they pulled back slightly, their fingers remained intertwined.

'How're things going?' Hailey asked.

Sasha's expression turned serious as she sighed, the weight of her recent struggles evident in her eyes. 'I've reached breaking point with my mother, Hailey. I'm actually considering involving social services.'

Hailey's eyebrows lifted. 'Social services? That's a big step.'

'I know, but I need to do something.' Sasha turned to look at her. 'Don't you think I should?'

Pausing for a moment, Hailey chose her words carefully. 'Sasha, it's a decision only you can make. Just make sure you know what you're getting yourself into.'

Sasha nodded. 'I know it won't be easy, but it's better than me constantly moaning about things and not actually doing anything about it.'

'Yeah, I know what you mean. That's why I left Christine's and moved into a hostel.'

Sasha's surprise was evident. 'A hostel? Why?'

Hailey shrugged, her smile slightly rueful. 'I just wanted my own space, I guess. It's time I stood on my own two feet.'

'Me too.' Sasha suddenly smiled. 'Does that mean I can come and stay over?'

'Afraid not. No overnight visitors are allowed.'

Sasha's disappointment was short-lived as Hailey's expression brightened.

'But I have another idea if you're interested.'

Sasha grinned as she pulled her into an embrace. 'Go on …'

Chapter Forty-Six

Lindsay's fingertips lightly trailed along the edge of the whisky glass, her gaze fixed on Josh as he poured a generous measure of amber liquid for himself. The low hum of their luxurious living room seemed to underscore the gravity of their conversation.

'He found me.' Josh's voice finally broke the silence, weariness evident in his tone.

He placed a small bag on the coffee table, the loud thud of it startling Lindsay.

Lindsay's eyes flicked to the bag, her heart pounding as anxiety churned within her.

'He found you?' Lindsay's voice was edged with disbelief. 'Where?'

Josh's gaze met hers, his eyes holding a resolute resolve. 'He came to the school.'

Lindsay's fingers tightened around the whisky glass, the cool surface offering a stark contrast to the emotions that swirled within her. Miles, the embodiment of their past mistakes and buried secrets, was no longer a phantom haunting their thoughts; he was tangible, within their reach.

Josh unzipped the bag, revealing a stack of cash neatly arranged inside. 'He wants money to keep quiet. This should be enough to ensure his cooperation.'

Lindsay's gaze flickered to the money, her mind racing with the implications of what they were about to do. It wasn't just money they were offering; it was a bargaining chip to keep the lid on the Pandora's box of their past.

As the silence lingered between them, Josh poured himself another drink and took a sip, his eyes locked on Lindsay's. 'I'm going to meet him tonight,' he said, his voice steady. 'He's promised to leave us alone once he gets this.'

Lindsay was fully aware that the secrets they harboured could shatter her career. But would this be enough to save it?

'I know this is all our savings, but you'll make it back with your new book, won't you?' he said.

Lindsay nodded slowly, her decision made. 'Yes. Just do it.'

As Josh's gaze held hers, Lindsay realised that they were standing on the edge of a precipice, about to confront the ghosts of their past and determine the course of their future.

With a heavy exhale, Lindsay raised her glass in a toast, a silent acknowledgment of the path they were embarking upon. The fate of their world now rested in the balance, and there was no turning back.

Chapter Forty-Seven

Sasha moved silently through her house, the floorboards creaking softly under her cautious steps. In her arms, she cradled a quilt and a stack of pillows.

Outside, the cool night air embraced Sasha as she made her way to Hailey's car parked at the kerb and climbed in.

'Hey there, sneaky,' Hailey said, her eyes sparkling mischievously.

Sasha's lips curved into a smile as she threw the quilt and pillows behind her, 'Hey yourself.'

'That looks awesome,' Sasha said, briefly looking over her shoulder.

The back seats had been folded down, creating a makeshift bed.

The engine hummed to life as Hailey started the car and guided them through the quiet streets. The world outside was shrouded in darkness, the occasional streetlight casting pools of gentle light. It felt like a secret adventure, a stolen moment away from the chaos of their lives.

The car came to a stop at a secluded area close to the park, and nearby, the swings swayed in the breeze as if welcoming them back. They exited the car and got into the back, arranging the quilt and pillows, turning the back of the car into a sanctuary of comfort.

Sasha rested her head against Hailey's chest, the

steady rhythm of her heartbeat a soothing backdrop to their conversation.

'So have you decided what you're gonna do about social services?' Hailey asked.

Sasha sighed softly. 'No. Every time I think I'm strong enough to call them, I see Chloe's little innocent face in my mind, and I can't help but wonder if things would be worse for her. I mean, she's got me—'

'But you're not her mother, Sasha. What're you gonna do, give up your life to raise her for the next eighteen years? What about all your dreams of travelling the world?'

'I know. I didn't say it was easy.'

Hailey leaned down and kissed her. 'That's why I love you, you're so selfless and—'

Sasha shifted into an upright position, her eyes locking onto Hailey's. 'Whoa, what did you say?'

A playful twinkle danced in Hailey's eyes. 'That you're selfless and—'

'No, not that part, the bit before.'

Hailey grinned. 'That I love you? I thought that was obvious.'

Leaning forward, Sasha bridged the distance between them and captured Hailey's lips in a lingering kiss. 'I've wanted to tell you I love you for ages.'

'So why didn't you?'

Sasha's fingers traced a tender path along Hailey's cheek. 'In case I scared you off.'

Hailey laughed. 'How could you? The most amazing, sexiest, most beautiful, kindest woman scare me off? I thank my lucky stars that I met you, and so would a million other women, which is why I'm never going to let you go.'

'Never?'

'Never, ever, ever.'

'I'm gonna hold you to that.'

Hailey's eyebrows arched in playful anticipation. 'You wanna seal the deal?'

'With?'

Hailey tenderly lifted Sasha's top, her fingers grazing against the softness of her skin. 'Oh, I think by doing this, for starters.' She leaned over and planted featherlight kisses on Sasha's chest, her breath warm against Sasha's skin.

'Mmm, and what else?' Sasha exhaled softly.

Hailey eased Sasha back against the pillows. 'Depends on how long we've got until sunrise.'

Chapter Forty-Eight

The atmosphere held an unmistakable tension, causing Lindsay's skin to tingle with discomfort. Emily sat behind her desk with a cold gaze fixed on Lindsay.

'Sit down,' Emily said, her fingers tapping rhythmically on the polished wooden surface.

Lindsay took a seat, her palms moistening as she clasped her hands together in her lap. She tried to keep her expression composed, her façade of a survivor of child abuse firmly in place.

'Is there a problem, Emily?'

'Yes, Lindsay. Yes, there is. A very big one.'

Lindsay frowned. 'Oh?'

'We've been working together for years, and during that time, I'd like to believe I've treated you fairly.'

'Is that a statement or a question?'

Emily ignored her comment and continued. 'The one thing this company and I pride ourselves on is trust.'

Lindsay nodded, wondering where this was all going. She had a hairdresser's appointment and she wished Emily would spare her the boring drivel she was having to endure.

'Your stories resonate with readers, and your personal background has been a driving force behind your work.'

Lindsay nodded, her gaze steady as she met her agent's eyes. 'Yes, I agree, my past has certainly shaped my writing. Look, Emily, I'd appreciate if you just told me what the issue is. I have to take Chloe to the hospital for a very important procedure and—'

'I received a package this morning.' Emily's lips tightened into a thin line, her eyes narrowing as if assessing Lindsay's features.

'And …'

Emily reached into her drawer and brought out a padded A4 envelope. 'And it seems we have a problem, or should I say, you do.'

Lindsay stomach churned with dread. She felt a growing sense of unease as Emily slid the envelope in her direction.

'Do you know what's in there?'

'No, how could I?' Lindsay said, her tone carefully neutral.

'Why don't you take a look.'

It can't be. Did that little bitch…

As Lindsay picked up the envelope and tentatively pulled out the papers, she knew exactly what was inside: the diary that had gone missing from her office. Though her mind was a whirlwind of panic and desperation, she made a show of looking like she was only seeing it for the first time.

Emily leaned forward, her gaze piercing through Lindsay's mask. 'Do you want to explain this to me?'

'I … I don't understand,' Lindsay stammered,

her fingers gripping the edge of her chair.

Emily's eyes remained fixed on her, unyielding. 'I think you understand perfectly well. It's time to come clean. Are your stories based on your reality, or someone else's?'

'I ...' Lindsay's voice wavered, her throat constricting as she struggled to find the right words.

'Are you going to tell me the truth?'

'After all I did for her, this is the thanks I get ...' Lindsay's voice broke, her eyes filling with tears. 'She said she'd make my life hell ...'

Emily frowned. 'I don't understand. Who did?'

'Hailey, the young woman I opened my home' – she paused for dramatic effect – 'and heart to.'

Lindsay rummaged in her bag for a tissue and dabbed her eyes, careful not to smudge her makeup.

'I've been so busy with Chloe lately while trying to make sure I don't let you down and meet deadlines, I asked Hailey to transcribe while I dictated.'

Emily's gaze softened slightly, her lips twitching in what could almost be mistaken for sympathy. 'Are you saying she doctored your notes?'

Lindsay nodded, tears freely streaming down her face. 'That's exactly what I'm saying. She's added things to make it look like I've plagiarised the work.'

'Why on earth would she do such a thing?'

Lindsay hesitated. 'Because I ... asked her to leave after I found out that she had blackmailed my daughter into sleeping with her. She'd been taking pictures of her in the shower without her knowledge, threatening to send them to her friends and put them online.'

Lindsay glanced at Emily to check whether or not she was buying her story. It was far-fetched, but the bigger the lie, the easier to believe. By the look of shock on Emily's face, she had clearly bought it hook, line and sinker.

'That's dreadful, Lindsay. Poor Sasha.'

'I know. I blame myself. I only wanted to help out a lady from church. I should've listened to Josh. He warned me about letting such a troubled girl into our lives but I ignored him.'

'You did nothing wrong, Lindsay. I knew there was an explanation behind this.'

Lindsay gave a small, weak smile. 'Thank you for your support.'

'All I'll need is for you to write a statement saying what you've told me, just to cover our backs. I hope you understand.'

'Of course. I'd be happy to.'

'Good. Once that's done, you can get back to producing more brilliant work.'

'I will.'

An hour later, Lindsay stormed out of the office building. The encounter had left her shaken. Her carefully constructed world of lies and deceit had nearly teetered on the brink of collapse. A white-hot rage consumed her as she scanned the area until seeing Josh's car parked just a short distance away. She strode towards the car, yanked open the car door, and slid into the passenger seat, her breath coming in harsh, ragged bursts. Josh glanced at her, his brow furrowing.

'Lindsay, what happened in there? You look furious.'

She clenched her fists as she struggled to contain her anger. 'I told you that fucking bitch took that diary. Not only did she steal it, she had the audacity to send it to my agent.'

Josh gave her an incredulous look. 'You're joking?'

'Do I look like I'm fucking joking?'

Josh's eyes narrowed. 'What did she say? Have you lost the book deal?'

Lindsay's chest heaved with frustration, her voice seething with suppressed rage. 'No, thank god. Emily was stupid enough to believe the spiel I came out with.'

Josh's grip tightened on the steering wheel, his gaze thoughtful as he considered their predicament. 'So what now?'

'Nothing. We're out of the woods for now. I just need to make sure neither of them step out of line again.'

'And how're you going to do that?'

'I have a plan.'

Josh looked at her questioningly.

'You'll have to wait and see.'

Lindsay knew that the decisions she made in the coming days would determine not only her fate but also the fate of those who dared to cross her.

Chapter Forty-Nine

Jo's hand trembled as she slowly placed the phone on the coffee table. The conversation had been a roller coaster of emotions, carrying her from hope to disappointment in a matter of minutes. She had believed that exposing Lindsay's true nature would be the catalyst for justice, the long-awaited crack in the façade that would finally bring her down. But the voice on the other end of the line had shattered that illusion, leaving Jo with a bitter taste of defeat.

The room felt heavy, suffocating almost, as she sank into an armchair. Her gaze was fixed on the drink she had poured herself, the amber liquid dancing gently in the glass. As she lifted it to her lips, the burn of alcohol did little to soothe her frustrations. Lindsay, like a chameleon, seemed to escape unscathed from every situation she caused, while those around her suffered the consequences.

Lindsay had always possessed an uncanny ability to wriggle out of tight spots, to dance through the raindrops of controversy without ever getting wet. Jo had witnessed it time and again: scandals that should have been career-ending stumbling blocks for anyone else, Lindsay had always emerged with her reputation not only intact, but often enhanced. It was maddening.

A bitter chuckle escaped Jo's lips as she set the glass down with a clink. Jo's disappointment had momentarily dampened her fighting spirit, but it was not extinguished. She knew she couldn't let Lindsay's victories deter her from exposing the truth.

Lindsay might have won this round, but Jo was not one to back down easily. The fire in her stomach reignited, fuelled by a newfound determination. She leaned forward, resting her elbows on her knees, her mind considering the possibilities.

There had to be another solution, a strategy that would chip away at Lindsay's defences until they crumbled.

All she had to do was find it.

Chapter Fifty

Sasha sat in the living room, her fingers idly tracing the pages of a book spread open on her lap. The words blurred before her as her thoughts spiralled away from the text, onto the events of the previous night. One that had left an indelible mark on her heart. Sasha's gaze drifted past the pages as she recalled the soft moonlight, the gentle rustle of leaves, and the warmth of Hailey's body against hers. The memory of Hailey's voice, filled with love, echoed in her ears, as she had spoken the words Sasha had longed to hear: 'I love you.'

And in that moment, the walls Sasha had built around herself came crashing down. It was liberating, like stepping out from the shadows into the light. Sasha's heart had swelled with emotions she hadn't known she was capable of feeling. Which was not surprising, having been brought up by a mother who was distant and cold, always more focused on appearances than emotions. Love had been a rare currency, hoarded rather than freely given.

And her father had only ever been present in the physical sense. His emotional absence had carved a void that had never truly been filled. The hollowness of his unavailability had left its mark on Sasha, imprinting a longing for something deeper, something real.

But Hailey had changed everything. In her, Sasha had found a confidante, a kindred spirit who saw past the façade she had perfected. Hailey's love had shattered the notion that affection was a weakness. It had shown Sasha that vulnerability was a strength, that opening her heart was not an invitation for pain but an opportunity for growth.

Sasha's thoughts drifted back to the present as a sigh escaped her lips. The book lay forgotten in her lap, her mind consumed by the memories and emotions that tugged at her heart. Tonight, she had plans to meet Hailey again – to be together under the vast canvas of the night sky – and she couldn't wait. She imagined the moment she would fall asleep in Hailey's arms once more, even if it was in the back of a car. The setting didn't matter; it was her presence that counted.

Oh god, she's back. Sasha braced herself. *What drama does she have up her sleeve today?*

Lindsay's steps were deliberate as she entered the room, her lips curved into an insincere smile as she dropped a stack of papers onto the nearby table.

Sasha frowned as she looked at the papers, a sense of foreboding settling in her chest. She picked up the forms, and her eyes widened as the truth of their contents hit her. They were adoption papers for Chloe. The words on the pages blurred together as her mind struggled to process the gravity of the situation.

'What's this?' Sasha's voice trembled.

She glanced up at Lindsay, her heart pounding as she tried to make sense of the sudden turn of events.

Lindsay's gaze remained steady, a veneer of icy calm masking the storm of emotions underneath.

'Adoption papers. I'm offering you a choice.'

'What choice?' Sasha's hands trembled slightly as she looked back down at the forms.

'I won't sign these papers,' Lindsay continued, her voice carrying a sinister undertone, 'if you agree to back up my story about Hailey stealing my jewellery.'

'What are you talking about? Hailey didn't steal anything!'

'If I said she did, then she did.'

The doorbell rang.

'Ah, just in time. So, what's it going to be? Your lesbian lover or your sweet little innocent sister? You haven't got long to decide.'

Oh my god, she knows I'm gay! Why hasn't she said anything until now?

To Sasha's surprise she no longer cared what her mother thought. Sasha was who she was. It wasn't as if her mother could dislike her any more than she already did.

Lindsay went to the door and came back moments later with two police officers.

Sasha's breath caught, her mind racing to grasp the situation.

The police? What the hell is my mother up to?

Lindsay's demeanour had shifted seamlessly, her expression now one of sadness and despair as she spun a web of lies about her stolen jewellery.

The false accusation sent shockwaves through Sasha, her mind struggling to comprehend the extent of Lindsay's manipulation.

Lindsay soon turned the spotlight onto Sasha. Her chest tightened as the officers' scrutiny bore down on her. She met their gaze, torn between the instinct to protect Chloe and the fear of the consequences of exposing Lindsay's deceit.

'Tell them how Hailey confessed to taking my jewellery, Sasha.' Lindsay placed a loving arm around Sasha. 'It's okay. The police are here to help.'

Sasha felt trapped, unsure of how to untangle herself without causing harm to Chloe or Hailey.

'Come on, darling, the officers haven't got all day, not to mention my plans for Chloe.'

There was an edge to her last words, and she knew if Lindsay had come this far, she would go even further.

Tears welled up in her eyes as the reality of what she was about to do settled in.

She was going to betray Hailey.

Chapter Fifty-One

Hailey stood in front of the mirror, carefully adjusting the collar of her shirt. A nervous excitement danced in the pit of her stomach as she applied a final touch of lipstick and checked her reflection one last time. As she turned away from the mirror, a knock on her door sent a jolt of surprise through her. It wasn't a gentle tap. It was sharp, more urgent. Hailey crossed the room and opened the door. Standing outside were two police officers, their expressions solemn.

Hailey's heart began to race as worry crept into her mind. 'Yeah?'

The older of the two officers spoke. 'Are you Hailey Summers?'

Hailey nodded. 'Is something wrong?'

The officer exchanged a glance with his colleague before returning his attention to Hailey.

'Miss Summers, you're under arrest on suspicion of theft,' the officer stated firmly, her voice devoid of emotion.

Hailey's heart sank as the weight of the accusation settled over her. Lindsay had actually gone through with her threat. She looked past the officers, her eyes locking onto the curious stares of other residents who had gathered in the hallway to witness the scene. They let her grab her jacket before they escorted Hailey to the police car. As the car drove through the streets, she searched for a way to get herself out of this. All they had was Lindsay's word. Hailey knew Lindsay's status held some weight, but surely they wouldn't charge her for something she didn't do.

They arrived at the police station, a large, imposing building with an exterior that seemed to demand respect. Hailey was led inside and down a corridor to a small interview room. The room was stark and sterile, with a table at the centre and two chairs on opposite sides. The walls were devoid of decoration, save for a clock that ticked audibly, adding to the sense of tension. Hailey tried to remain calm as she waited to be questioned.

'Miss Summers, let's get straight to the point,' Detective Simmons began, her voice cutting through the silence. 'We have reason to believe that you were involved in the theft of valuable jewellery from Lindsay's home.'

'No, I didn't steal anything! Lindsay's lying because I'm dating her daughter Sasha—'

Detective Simmons raised a hand, cutting her off. 'The same daughter who has corroborated her mother's claims.'

Hailey's heart shattered at the mention of Sasha's betrayal. She had trusted Sasha, believed in their connection, and now it seemed like she had let her down – pretty much like everyone in her life. After what felt like an eternity, the interview finally came to an end and she made her way towards the exit, having been bailed pending further enquiries.

As she descended the steps, she spotted Sasha standing there. Hailey's emotions were a tumultuous storm inside her, a whirlwind of anger, hurt, and confusion that threatened to consume her. She couldn't ignore the fact that Sasha had played a role in landing her in this situation.

Sasha took a step forward. 'Hailey, please, let me explain.'

'Explain!? You sided with her, Sasha. After everything.'

Sasha's eyes welled up with tears, her voice cracking. 'I didn't know what to do. She said she was going to sign adoption papers …'

Hailey's anger flared, drowning out Sasha's words. 'So you just threw me under the bus?'

'No, it wasn't like that. I was scared. I—'

'And how'd you think I felt being held in a room and interrogated for something I didn't do?'

'I'm sorry, Hailey.' Sasha's voice was a desperate plea. 'I never meant for it to turn out like this.'

Hailey shook her head. 'I can't believe I trusted you. I can't believe you did this to me.'

Sasha reached out to touch Hailey's arm, but Hailey pulled away as if she had been burned. 'Don't touch me. Just leave me alone.'

Sasha's face crumpled, tears streaming down her cheeks. 'Hailey, please, don't shut me out. I love you, and I messed up, but I want to make it right.'

But Hailey was done listening. 'You've made your choice. I hope it was worth it.'

Turning away, Hailey walked off. She wiped away her tears, refusing to let Sasha see the extent of the damage she had caused.

Chapter Fifty-Two

Sasha's heartache and frustration led her straight to the doorstep of the one person who had always been her rock: Aunt Jo. She needed guidance, a source of strength and reason in the midst of the chaos her life had become. With a heavy heart, Sasha found herself sitting across from Jo, recounting the painful events that had unfolded at the police station. Jo listened attentively as Sasha poured out her emotions and the depth of her hurt.

'I can't believe your mother put you in that position,' Jo said.

'I don't know why I went along with it. I know what my mother's like; I should've called her bluff and refused to get involved,' Sasha admitted.

Jo's gaze was steady and sympathetic as she reached out to gently place a hand over Sasha's. 'You did what you thought was best at the time.'

Tears welled up in Sasha's eyes as she struggled to keep her emotions in check. 'And now my mum knows that all she needs to do is wave that form in front of me and I'll do whatever she says. What do I do now, Aunt Jo? I can never forgive her for this. In the same way, Hailey will never forgive me either.'

Jo sighed, her expression thoughtful. 'Give Hailey a few days to calm down. She's probably very angry right now and just needs some space. She's got every right to feel the way she does, but hopefully she'll understand why you did it once the fog clears.'

'I hope you're right. I bet my dad knew about all this; he's such a wimp,' Sasha said, a touch of frustration in her voice.

Jo got to her feet and walked over to the window. 'That's what I thought, but he's trying to make amends. I finally think, after all these years, he's seeing the light.'

Sasha snorted. 'He wouldn't see the light if you shone a torch straight into his eyes.'

Jo turned. 'That's where you're wrong.'

'I'll believe it when I see it.'

'Sasha, I didn't want to tell you this until I knew the outcome, but it seems it backfired anyway.'

'What did?'

'Your dad found a diary in your mum's office, Hailey's diary—'

'My mum had Hailey's diary? I don't believe this! Why would she invade her privacy like that? That's so sick.'

'I totally agree.'

A sudden thought hit Sasha. 'So that's what she was accusing me of stealing? It was my dad that took it, but why?'

'Did you know your mum is writing a new book?'

'Yeah, but she won't tell me what it's about. It's top secret or something.'

'Well, I can tell you. She's writing her biography.'

Sasha let out a laugh. 'What's it called, *Memoirs of the Wicked Witch of the East*?'

'No,' Jo said in all seriousness. 'It's about her life growing up in foster care.'

Sasha shook her head. 'Aunt Jo, my mum didn't grow up in—' She stopped mid-sentence, her hand clasping her mouth. 'Please don't tell me she's stolen Hailey's story and made it her own.'

'I'm afraid she has. Your dad sent the diary to her agent—'

Sasha tilted her head. 'He did?'

'Yes, but it turned out to be a pointless gesture. Lindsay spun some yarn about Hailey having it in for her and doctoring her notes.'

'Oh my god, so that's why she had Hailey arrested? To punish me because she thought I sent the diary to her agent?'

'Probably.'

Sasha pushed herself to her feet. 'I need to have a word with that woman before things get even more out of hand.'

With a determined resolve, Sasha made her way back home. Lindsay was in her office, happily typing away about Hailey's life.

'What are you doing here? I thought you were at university.'

'You expect me to be able to study after what you did yesterday?' Sasha said, anger and hurt seeping into her words.

'All I did was come through on a promise I made. I told you to stay away from her, but you wouldn't listen—'

'And why's that? Were you scared that if she stayed here, she'd find out the truth about you stealing her life and trying to make it look like your own? Do you really think you're going to get away with it?'

Lindsay smiled. 'I already have. Hailey has no credibility; you yourself called her a thief.'

'Only because you made me do it.'

'Really? It didn't take much to throw your girlfriend under the bus, did it? All those whispers of sweet nothings in her diary nearly made me vomit. Anyone would think you're the lesbian version of Romeo and Juliet.'

Sasha opened her mouth to respond, but Lindsay held up her hand to silence her.

'Sasha, your actions have consequences. You need to take responsibility for what you've done and understand the impact of your choices.'

It was a painful truth, but it was a necessary one to make Sasha realise her mother hadn't held a gun to her head.

But she hadn't exactly put up much of a fight either.

Chapter Fifty-Three

Hailey sat alone at the bar. Her fingers traced the rim of her half-empty glass, the transparent liquid inside reflecting the light in fractured patterns. She had sought solace in the embrace of alcohol, hoping it would numb the ache that had settled deep within her heart.

As the minutes turned into hours, Hailey's gaze remained distant, lost in her thoughts. The weight of recent events bore down on her, each sip of her drink attempting to drown the pain that seemed insurmountable.

The sound of a stool scraping against the floor pulled Hailey's attention away from her glass. Christine settled onto the seat next to her, her expression full of concern and empathy. She placed a gentle hand on Hailey's shoulder.

'Hey,' Christine said.

Hailey turned her head to look at her, a half-hearted smile tugging at her lips. 'Hey, Chris.'

'You okay?' Christine's eyes searched Hailey's face.

Hailey's laugh was bitter. 'Do I look okay?'

Christine's hand squeezed Hailey's shoulder gently. 'Wanna talk about it?'

Hailey sighed. 'Sasha ... she ... she betrayed me, Chris.'

'What happened?'

Tears welled up in Hailey's eyes, threatening to

spill over. She took a shaky breath, her voice cracking as she recounted the painful ordeal. 'She lied to the police. She backed up her mother's story and accused me of stealing. I was arrested. I trusted her, and she … she threw me under the bus.'

'I'm so sorry, Hailey. I can't imagine how much that must hurt.'

Hailey nodded, her throat tight. 'I thought we had something real, you know? Something special.'

Christine placed a comforting hand over Hailey's. 'Sometimes people make mistakes, especially under pressure. Maybe she was scared or didn't know how to handle it.'

Hailey's gaze dropped to her glass, the liquid inside swaying with her unsteady hand. 'I get that, but to lie about me like that? To make me look like a criminal? I don't know if I can forgive her.'

Christine's voice was gentle, filled with understanding. 'Maybe it's time to pull back from the relationship for a while. Take a break to clear your head and see where things stand.'

'I don't know. The thought of being without her hurts too.'

'How about this? Why don't you come stay with me for the weekend? A change of scenery might help, and you could use some time away from all this.'

Hailey considered the offer, torn between her pain and the need to find some semblance of peace. 'I appreciate it. I really do. But I think I just need some time alone right now.'

Christine nodded, her smile understanding. 'Of course. Just know that I'm here for you, no matter what.'

Tears glistened in Hailey's eyes. 'Thank you. It means more than you know.'

As the evening wore on, Hailey's glass emptied, and the weight of her heartache only seemed to deepen. She watched as Christine left the bar, a sense of solitude settling around her. The ache remained, but somewhere deep within her, she clung to the hope that time might heal the wounds, that the shattered pieces of her heart might one day mend.

Chapter Fifty-Four

Lindsay's fingers tapped impatiently on the steering wheel as she navigated the city streets. She had successfully traced Hailey's current residence, and with a newfound sense of power, she intended to exploit the situation to her advantage.

Parking in front of the hostel, Lindsay took a moment to collect herself. She needed to project an air of control. Stepping out of the car, she strode purposefully towards the entrance, the click of her heels echoing on the pavement.

Inside, Lindsay approached the front desk. Her enquiry for Hailey's room number was initially met with reluctance. However, after Lindsay disclosed she was famous and offered to take a selfie, the receptionist eagerly shared the information, clearly thrilled at meeting a celebrity.

Lindsay ascended the stairs, rehearsing the words she would use to manipulate the situation. She located Hailey's door, knocked, and awaited a response.

The door opened, revealing Hailey's surprised expression that quickly shifted to anger.

'What do you want?'

'I have an offer for you.'

Arms crossed defensively, Hailey's voice was sharp. 'I'm not interested in anything you have to offer.'

'I think you might want to hear this one. You

see, I have a proposition that could benefit both of us.'

'I highly doubt that.'

Closing the gap, Lindsay said, 'You're in a predicament right now, aren't you? Facing charges for something you didn't do. I can make those charges disappear.'

Hailey's eyes narrowed. 'And what's the catch?'

Lindsay brushed past Hailey and entered the room. She waited until Hailey closed the door before she spoke.

'I want your life story so I can pass it off as my own.'

Hailey's gaze hardened. 'You must be out of your mind if you think I'd agree to that.'

Maintaining her composure, Lindsay locked eyes with Hailey. 'Consider it. Your freedom in exchange for my control over the narrative.'

'You're asking me to sacrifice my truth so you get to play the victim.'

'If you want to put it like that, yes. You see, I need some insurance that all of this won't come back and bite me in the arse. My darling daughter sent my agent your diary that I copied and—'

'You read my diary?'

'Yes, it was a fascinating read, hence why you can see my need for it.'

'No! What? You're crazier than I thought you were.'

'No, not crazy. Ambitious. I always get what I want. So, what d'you say? You tell my agent that you doctored my notes and I tell the police there was a big misunderstanding and that I simply misplaced my jewellery, then we all go our separate ways.'

Silence hung between them, the weight of the decision palpable. Hailey's mind raced as she grappled with the magnitude of the proposition.

'Fine,' Hailey's voice spat out. 'I'll do it.'

Lindsay's smile widened, victory apparent. 'Good. I thought you might see reason. Oh, and one more thing. Think of it as a little bonus. I need you to write some info about your foster parents' backgrounds. Make sure it's controversial. My readers love a bit of a sob story.'

As Lindsay turned to leave, Hailey's voice followed her.

'Make no mistake, Lindsay. This isn't over.'

Walking away, Lindsay's steps exuded confidence. While Hailey might have agreed to her terms, Lindsay was well aware that the battle was far from over.

Sat in the comfort of her car, she called Emily.

'Hello?'

'Hi, Emily, it's Lindsay,' she stated coolly.

'Lindsay, how have you been?'

Lindsay's smile was calculated, even though Emily couldn't see it. 'I've spoken to Hailey and she's seen sense at last. She's horrified at the inconvenience she caused and so is going to write her own statement admitting to what she did.'

'That would be a massive weight off my mind.'

'I thought it would be.' Lindsay's confidence

radiated. 'There won't be any more issues with this book.'

'Wonderful. I look forward to reading your next chapters.'

Satisfaction filled Lindsay as the call ended. With Hailey in her grasp and her agent's commitment, she felt certain that her secrets would remain concealed, and her reputation unblemished.

Chapter Fifty-Five

'Hailey, wait!' Sasha's voice carried a sense of urgency. Hailey's stomach churned. She didn't want to confront Sasha, didn't want to face the feelings that still caused her pain every time she thought of her.

Hailey slowed, turning reluctantly to find Sasha running towards her, her expression desperate. Hailey's guard remained firmly in place.

'What do you want now?'

'I know you're angry. And you have every right to be. But please, I have something to tell you.'

Hailey's jaw tightened. 'Fine. Make it quick.'

Sasha's breath caught as she gathered her thoughts. 'I need you to know that I never wanted any of this to happen. I never wanted you to get hurt.'

'You've already said that, and I'm not interested. I thought you had something to tell me.'

Sasha nodded, her voice quickening as she spoke. 'My mother ... She stole your diary. She's writing a biography and using your story as her own.'

Hailey managed a bitter smile, her cynicism taking over. 'Already ahead of you. She paid me a visit, offered to drop the charges if I keep quiet.'

Sasha sighed, her remorse evident. 'I'm so sorry, Hailey. I never imagined she would stoop this low. I never meant for any of this to happen.'

A sense of sadness welled up within Hailey, but

she held it back, her walls firmly in place. 'Sorry, doesn't change anything.'

'I miss you. Every day without you feels empty.'

For a fleeting moment, Hailey's resolve wavered. The ache of their separation tugged at her heart, reminding her of the connection they once shared. But she quickly steadied herself, refusing to let vulnerability overtake her.

'I have to go.'

'Will I see you again?'

Hailey continued walking, her steps deliberate and resolute. The question hung in the air. But Hailey couldn't bring herself to answer. As the distance between them grew, she knew that the path ahead was filled with uncertainty, and the fractured pieces of their relationship might never fully mend.

Arriving at the local library, Hailey walked with purpose towards the real-life stories section. Reaching the shelves, she began to browse through the selection of books, each one representing a real-life account of triumph, tragedy, and resilience. She selected a stack that spanned various genres and experiences, knowing that within these pages lay the inspiration she needed to craft a narrative that would captivate and expose Lindsay's true nature.

With her arms laden with books, Hailey found a quiet corner of the library. She settled into a chair, a notebook and pen beside her.

Hours passed as Hailey meticulously took notes, jotting down poignant quotes, details of personal struggles, and moments of triumph.

As she worked, a smile crossed her lips. She had a plan, a plan that would allow her to turn the tables on Lindsay in the most spectacular way. She was going to give Lindsay a story so compelling, so masterfully crafted, that it would expose the depths of her manipulation and deceit.

Chapter Fifty-Six

Jo stood by her front door, her gaze steady and expectant as she watched Miles approach. As he reached her doorstep, Jo held out her arms to him. He hesitated for a moment before stepping into her embrace.

'I've dreamed of this day, Miles,' she whispered.

He remained silent as he drew back, a mixture of emotions playing across his face.

'I wasn't expecting you until later. Your dad said he wasn't meeting you until tonight,' Jo said.

'Lindsay switched up the times. She's a busy bee, that one,' Miles replied.

Jo grinned. 'She's going to be even busier soon. Did your dad give it to you?'

'Got it all right here,' Miles said, stepping over the threshold and into Jo's home. The bag in his hand seemed to carry a weight, and Jo's gaze remained fixed on it as he opened it, revealing the contents within.

'Wow, I've never seen so much money in my life.'

'You want some?' Miles said, dipping his hand into the bag and withdrawing a wad of money.

Jo pushed his hand away. 'No, that's for the three of you. You all deserve it.'

'Nothing beats family.'

'I can attest to that, Miles. And I promise nothing is going to tear this family apart again. Nothing.'

Despite the tough exterior he had displayed, there was a vulnerability about him that she understood all too well.

He offered a small nod, his gaze lingering on Jo as if he were searching for something more within her understanding eyes. There was a sense of closure in this encounter, a chapter finally coming to an end.

'I never forgot you, you know,' Miles said, his voice sincere.

Jo smiled gently, her hand reaching out to rest on his shoulder. 'Likewise. This will all be over soon, and we can be like a real family again.'

'Any chance you can get Sasha to come over? I'd like to meet her properly.'

Jo took out her phone. 'Consider it done.'

Chapter Fifty-Seven

In a small coffee shop nestled on a tranquil street, Hailey sat across from Christine, the comforting scent of freshly brewed coffee enveloping them. Feeling the pressure of everything closing in, Hailey realised it was time to reveal the whole truth to Christine.

'I hope you won't judge me when I say this,' Hailey began earnestly, 'but I need to tell you what's been really happening.'

Christine leaned in slightly. 'You can always talk to me. I'm here to listen.'

Taking a deep breath, Hailey steadied herself, her fingertips tracing the edge of her coffee cup as she gathered her thoughts. She recounted the unfolding events, from Lindsay's blackmail to the involvement of the police, leaving no detail unspoken.

'It's just,' Hailey continued, her gaze unwaveringly fixed on Christine, 'I can't get over how manipulative she is. How could she use her own daughter to support her lies.'

Christine's focus shifted to her cup of coffee. Hailey observed her closely, sensing an inner conflict brewing beneath the surface.

'Don't blame yourself for bringing us together,' Hailey said gently. 'You only did what you thought was right. You are the complete opposite to her – honest to a fault.'

Christine cleared her throat, still avoiding eye contact. 'You're right. Honesty is a cornerstone.'

Hailey detected a hint of unease. 'Is something worrying you?'

'No, it's just …'

Growing more concerned, Hailey pressed on. 'You can tell me anything.'

At last, Christine looked up, her eyes meeting Hailey's. 'I might not be the person you think I am. People, well, sometimes I make mistakes – complex ones. Mistakes that can impact someone's life.'

Hailey's heart sank as the implication of Christine's words settled in. A knot of tension formed in her stomach, and she grappled with another betrayal. 'Christine, have you … lied to me?'

Christine let out a weary sigh. 'I can't deny that I've, at times, withheld certain information. But it's always been with the intention of safeguarding you, Hailey. Shielding you from pain.'

Confusion clouded Hailey's mind. She had always trusted Christine, confided in her, and now she was grappling with the realisation that their friendship might not be what she thought it was.

'Even if you had good intentions, it's still lying.'

'I'm aware,' Christine admitted, her voice laced with remorse. 'And I'm sorry.'

'So … what have you lied about?'

A glimmer of uncertainty flickered in Christine's eyes before she spoke. 'I'd rather not go into it now. Just believe me when I say it was in your best interests.'

As they sat there, the unspoken thoughts lingered between them, a palpable reminder that even the closest bonds could be marred by hidden truths. Hailey couldn't help but wonder what exactly Christine might be keeping from her.

Chapter Fifty-Eight

Sasha stood across the street from Hailey's hostel, her heart heavy with grief. How did it all come to this? How did she allow things to spiral so far out of control?

Thoughts swirled in her mind, a tempest of memories and what-ifs that threatened to drown her. If only she could turn back time, reverse the choices that led her down this painful path.

She thought she was protecting Chloe, doing what was right. But the cost was astronomical – her connection with Hailey, the trust they had once shared, shattered into irreparable fragments.

As she kept her gaze fixed on the hostel, movement caught her eye. Hailey's figure appeared in one of the windows, her silhouette framed by a light. Sasha's heart skipped a beat at the sight of her, a surge of emotions overwhelming her all at once.

Every fibre of her being urged her to rush to Hailey, to beg once more for her understanding, to explain the circumstances again that pushed her to act the way she had. Yet fear held her back, fear of rejection and the haunting notion that her actions might have forever altered their relationship.

Within the room, Hailey moved, her shadow shifting against the light. Sasha watched her lower the blinds, the room darkening like the prospects of mending their fractured bond. She had lost her, the person who meant more to her than she ever realised.

Tears welled in her eyes, blurring the view before her. Leaning against a tree, hidden from sight, she struggled to contain her emotions. If only she could rewind time, make different choices. But life rarely offered second chances.

Regret enveloped her like a suffocating fog, leaving her shivering in its grip. She had been manipulated by her own mother, manipulated into betraying the one person who truly mattered.

In the shadows, she stood alone, confronting the consequences of her actions. Silently, she wished for an opportunity to right her wrongs, to mend the fractures she had caused. But as she lingered in the darkness, she knew she had to find a way to make amends, to heal the wounds she had inflicted, and to strive for a chance to rebuild what was broken.

Chapter Fifty-Nine

Hailey's fingers hovered over her phone as she dialled Lindsay's number. Her heart raced, anxiety and determination coursing through her veins. She had prepared herself for this moment, meticulously crafting her notes and thoughts into a narrative that would ultimately give Lindsay exactly what she wanted: a story of hardship and struggle to pass off as her own.

They agreed to meet in Lindsay's car, parked in a secluded spot away from prying eyes. As Hailey slid her notes across the car's dashboard, she watched Lindsay's expression closely, searching for any trace of emotion. Lindsay's eyes scanned the pages, and Hailey could almost see the wheels turning in her mind as she absorbed the carefully constructed story.

Lindsay looked up, a smirk playing at the corners of her lips. 'If I actually cared, your life would seem pretty sad,' she remarked coolly.

Hailey's lips tightened, her frustration simmering beneath the surface. 'I did what you asked. Now call the police and retract your statement.'

A touch of amusement danced in Lindsay's eyes as she picked up her phone and made the call, her words curt and to the point. Once she ended the call, she leaned back in her chair, her eyes fixing on Hailey once more.

'Why did you do all this?' Hailey's voice trembled

in anger. 'The lies, taking me in … What was the point?'

Lindsay's laughter was almost chilling, devoid of any genuine amusement. 'Because I could,' she replied with a shrug. 'It was all for show, Hailey. A carefully crafted façade to make myself look like a saviour.'

'Why did you have a baby that you didn't want to look after?'

Lindsay's gaze flickered, a hint of discomfort crossing her features before she looked away. 'Ah, Chloe. She was an accident,' she admitted. 'And by the time I realised it was a mistake, it was too late to do anything about it.'

'You had a child, a human being, and you treat her like an inconvenience.'

'That's because she is. Don't pretend you understand anything about me or my life,' Lindsay spat.

'Despite everything, I feel sorry for you,' Hailey said softly, her words sincere.

Lindsay's laughter rang out again, but this time, it held a touch of bitterness. 'Save your pity. Soon enough, I'll be the perfect victim in the story I tell the world.'

Hailey climbed out the car.

'I hope this is the last time we'll be seeing each other,' Lindsay said.

I doubt it very much!

Hailey smiled as she closed the door. When Lindsay's car disappeared from view, Hailey took a deep breath. Her hand trembled slightly as she lowered her phone, which had been recording their conversation. A sense of empowerment and closure settled over her.

'Yes, Lindsay,' she muttered under her breath, looking at the recording. 'Soon, everyone will know your story, but it won't be the narrative you think.'

Chapter Sixty

Sasha's phone buzzed urgently. She glanced at the screen, her heart rate quickening as she read Jo's text message:

Sasha, can you come over? Urgent!

There was a frantic undertone to Jo's words that sent a shiver down her spine. Grabbing her jacket, she hurried out the door.

Arriving at Jo's house, she was met with a surprising sight. Miles was sitting on the sofa, his presence unexpected yet more than welcome.

'Thanks for coming, Sasha,' Jo's voice broke the silence, offering a small smile. 'I'm sorry if I worried you.'

Sasha shook her head, her gaze darting between Jo and Miles. 'It's okay. What's happening?'

Miles cleared his throat. 'I wanted to see you. Under better circumstances this time.'

'I'm glad.'

Years of unsaid words and separation lingered in the room.

Jo seemed to sense the awkwardness, stepping in with her characteristic insight. 'Let's talk. It's time we addressed things that have been buried for far too long.'

The conversation began hesitantly, the three of

them tiptoeing around the minefield of their shared past. Josh, who had left behind a legacy of confusion and pain, was at the heart of it. Stories, memories, and a newfound perspective on the intricate tapestry of their family began to unfurl.

As the evening wore on, the topic shifted to the one individual who had inflicted immeasurable suffering on all of them – Lindsay. Miles recounted his own battles with her as a child, stories that mirrored her own.

'Why did you decide to reappear in our lives now?' Sasha finally asked.

Miles met her gaze. 'I needed answers and closure. I wanted to understand our dad, our family's history. I wanted to meet you.'

Jo rose from her seat, retrieving an envelope from the table. She handed it to Sasha. 'This is for you. You and Miles both deserve a fresh start.'

Sasha looked inside the envelope, and gasped. 'Where did all this money come from?'

'Let's just say it's a gift from your father in an attempt to hide his past.'

Walking home that night, Sasha's heart felt lighter than it had in ages. She wished Hailey could have been there to share the moment, to be part of their reunion.

Gazing up at the stars, she couldn't help but hope that they could all find a way to heal, to emerge from the shadows of their past, and build a brighter, stronger future together.

Chapter Sixty-One

Lindsay sat on her sofa, a crystal flute of champagne in her hand, savouring the feeling of accomplishment that surged within her. The outline Hailey had given her had been meticulously crafted, every twist and turn calculated to ensnare readers in its narrative. The story she had woven was a tapestry of tragedy and triumph, threaded with her signature flair for drama. It represented the culmination of her efforts, the product of her creativity and cunning. Having sent it off for Emily's review, she anticipated a call from her agent later that afternoon. Confident in the authenticity of Hailey's experiences, Lindsay expected nothing less than glowing praise.

In a matter of months, she envisioned leaving her mundane life behind in the UK to embark on a worldwide book tour. She could picture herself gracing talk show stages, feigning tears of sorrow, resting in luxurious five-star hotels, and indulging in exquisite meals at Michelin-star restaurants. The world was poised to become her oyster, and she would be travelling lightly. Josh could handle the burden of raising Chloe; as for his son Miles, well, his fate was not her concern.

Lindsay's phone chimed, the familiar sound of a new email drawing her attention. Setting her champagne flute aside, she picked up her phone and let out a soft, anticipatory sigh.

'Come on, Emily, tell me how incredibly

marvellous I am,' she murmured under her breath.

With a swift motion, she opened the email, her eyes scanning the screen in search of praise. However, the words that met her gaze were anything but what she had expected.

Emily's email delivered a devastating blow, an abrupt and ruthless condemnation of Lindsay's actions. As she read the scathing words, her mind struggled to process the stark reality of the situation. Lindsay's carefully constructed façade crumbled before her eyes, leaving her stunned and disorientated.

With trembling fingers, she dialled Emily's number, the phone ringing twice before it was answered.

'Emily, I just received your email—'

'You've destroyed yourself, Lindsay. Your career is in ruins!' Emily's voice was cutting, each word a dagger to Lindsay's pride. 'You've not only engaged in plagiarism, but you had the audacity to plagiarise from *New York Times* bestsellers. Did my kindness make you think you could get away with this?'

'Emily, please, let me explain—'

'No, Lindsay! … Let me make it clear that by the end of today, the truth about your deceitful, conniving ways will be public knowledge. Your name will be tarnished beyond repair, to the point where self-publishing will be an unreachable dream.'

The line went dead, leaving Lindsay in stunned silence. Panic surged within her. How had everything gone so wrong? What options did she have to salvage the situation? The realization dawned on her: there might be no way out.

Driven by desperation, Lindsay rushed upstairs, barging into Sasha's room and collapsing to her knees beside her bed.

Tears welled up in Lindsay's eyes as she implored Sasha, her voice shaky and desperate. 'Sasha, please, help me. I've ruined everything, and I'm lost!'

'I can't help you, Mum. I'm sorry. You've taken everything from me, and I have nothing left to give.'

'Call your girlfriend and convince her to take the blame for this mess,' Lindsay pleaded, her desperation apparent. 'Tell her she can come back, you can share a room—'

'It's too late, Mum.' Sasha's voice held resignation. 'You've burned all your bridges. It's time for you to face the consequences, just as I've had to by losing Hailey.'

Struggling to her feet, Lindsay wiped away her tears with the back of her hand, smearing her makeup.

'You're to blame for all of this,' Lindsay snapped in anger, her voice seething with accusation. 'You probably put her up to this.'

'Of course, Mum, blame me for your lies.' Sasha's response was tinged with bitter irony. 'But in the end, the responsibility is yours, as it's always been.'

Sasha's expression remained resolute, a testament to the shattered bond between them. Lindsay had spun her intricate web of deceit, and now she was entangled in its threads, facing the consequences of her actions.

Chapter Sixty-Two

Wracked with guilt, Sasha's eyes remained downcast as she pushed through the glass door and walked down the corridor to the waiting room. If anyone glanced at her, they'd probably think she was just a normal, carefree teenager. Little did they know.

She followed the sign that led to the room she was searching for. Despite the early hour, the room was already packed. Stressed-out parents looked like they'd been through the wringer with their hyperactive kids. Some loners were buried in their phones, trying to tune out the chaos. Sasha went up to the reception desk, sneaking a nervous glance at the middle-aged woman with coal black hair and blue eyes stationed behind it.

'What can I do for you, hon?' the woman asked with a half-hearted smile.

Sasha questioned what she was about to do. This morning she had been so sure of her decision, but now, she felt like this whole thing was a huge mistake. How could she even think about doing this to Chloe?

As she turned to leave, something stopped her in her tracks. She quickly reminded herself why she was here – for Chloe, for her future. It wasn't a betrayal; it was a tough choice made out of love.

The words caught in her throat, a lump forming that seemed impossible to swallow. How could she even begin to explain this to the woman behind the desk? She wrestled with her thoughts, trying to find a way to put the turmoil in her heart into words.

She took a deep breath, gathering the scattered fragments of her courage.

'Um, it's about my sister,' she finally managed to say, her voice barely louder than a whisper.

The tired smile on the woman's face faded slightly, replaced by a gentle concern. 'Your sister? What's going on, sweetheart?'

Sasha's gaze briefly dropped to the floor. 'Well, it's just that my mum … she's been really neglecting my sister. She's just a baby, you know? And my mum's always busy with, like, everything else.'

The woman's expression softened even more, her eyes reflecting empathy and understanding.

'I'm really sorry to hear that,' she said softly. 'It must be really hard for both you and your sister.'

Sasha nodded, feeling a rush of emotions she had been bottling up for so long.

'Yeah, it's just … I don't know what to do anymore. I can't take care of her all the time, and I can't just stand by and watch her get ignored.'

The woman leaned in a little, her voice gentle. 'You're very brave for coming forward. It takes a lot to speak up about something like this.'

A tear escaped Sasha's eye, and she quickly brushed it away, frustrated by her own vulnerability. 'I just want things to be better for her. She deserves more than this.'

The woman nodded in agreement. 'We'll do our

best to help. It's important that kids have someone looking out for them.'

As Sasha absorbed her words, a sense of relief mingled with the lingering guilt. Opening up about her family's struggles was both terrifying and liberating. But maybe, just maybe, by breaking the silence, things could start to change for the better.

Chapter Sixty-Three

The days that followed Hailey's last encounter with Lindsay were a whirlwind of activity. With determination in her heart, Hailey set her plan into motion. Returning to the library, she delved into books on resilience, strength, and overcoming adversity. Armed with a pen and paper, she meticulously documented her thoughts, experiences, and aspirations. The library became a sanctuary, a space where she channelled her emotions and determination into something palpable.

The sting of Sasha's involvement in Lindsay's lies still lingered in Hailey's heart. She couldn't comprehend how Sasha had fallen under Lindsay's manipulative sway, but dwelling on it offered no solace. Hailey had exacted her revenge on Lindsay by exposing her deceit in an eloquent letter dropped off at her agent's office. Within twenty-four hours, Lindsay's cheating ways had trended on Twitter, and the exposé was still reverberating.

However, amid the chaos, Hailey found a renewed sense of purpose. She dedicated herself tirelessly to crafting a story outline that was uniquely hers. Eventually, the moment arrived when Hailey felt ready to share her story with the world.

Armed with her manuscript idea, Hailey took the next crucial step. She reached out to a literary agent, pitching her tale of triumph over adversity. The agent's intrigue was palpable, initiating discussions of potential publication. Hailey's journey had taken an unforeseen turn – from victim to author, from a pawn in Lindsay's game to the master of her own destiny.

Weeks had passed since Hailey had seen Sasha. Calls and texts had stopped, Sasha seemingly having absorbed the message. The reality saddened Hailey, but she recognised the inevitability of moving forward, of letting go.

One day, Hailey ventured to Jo's house to return some of Sasha's belongings left behind in her car. The thought of returning to Sasha's home, laden with painful memories, felt unbearable.

As Jo opened the door, a warm smile greeted Hailey.

'Hey there, Hailey.'

'Hi, Jo,' Hailey replied, handing over the bag.

'Don't rush off. Come on in and have a drink.'

Stepping inside, Hailey found herself enveloped in the familiarity of the space. She settled onto the sofa, her fingers interlacing in her lap.

'I've been doing well,' she said, meeting Jo's gaze.

'That's amazing,' Jo responded with genuine enthusiasm. 'A book deal, Hailey. That's incredible.'

'Yeah, it's an opportunity for me to share my story, to reclaim what Lindsay stole.'

Before parting ways, Hailey reached into her pocket. 'Before I go, there's something I want to give you.' She placed a small flash drive into Jo's hand.

Jo examined the flash drive, curiosity evident on

her face. 'What's this?'

'It's a recording,' Hailey explained. 'Lindsay admitting to everything she's done: her lies, her manipulation. It's evidence, Jo. Evidence that might help Sasha.'

'You recorded Lindsay?'

Hailey nodded. 'I did it for Sasha, in case she ever needs it. I didn't bring it before because I thought Lindsay's downfall would be enough.'

Tears welled in Jo's eyes as she looked at Hailey. She reached out, squeezing Hailey's hand. 'You and Sasha don't have to be apart. There's a way you can be together now.'

Confusion flickered across Hailey's face. 'What do you mean?'

Taking a deep breath, Jo said, 'Sasha reported Lindsay to social services. I'm sure this will be a great help.'

Hailey's eyes widened in surprise. 'Sasha called social services?'

'Yes, what Lindsay did to you was a wake-up call for Sasha. She's been devastated ever since.'

Hailey's emotions were a whirlwind – conflicted, raw, uncertain. 'I don't know if I can trust her again.'

'Start with your mind, Hailey. Let it pave the way. Lindsay caused a lot of pain, and we're all healing. Consider being part of that healing process with us.'

As Jo extended her offer, a spark of hope ignited within Hailey. Maybe there was a chance for her to find her version of happiness, even as she pursued her dreams.

'Just think about it,' Jo encouraged gently. 'That's all I'm asking.'

With Jo's words resonating, Hailey realised that amidst the intricacies of life, she could craft a new story – one of hope, redemption, and her own form of happiness.

Chapter Sixty-Four

Hailey hesitated for a moment before knocking on Christine's door. She hadn't seen her since the night at the bar, and Christine's admission had been playing on her mind. The door opened, and to her surprise, Robert stood there, looking as shocked as she was.

'Hey,' he greeted, his voice tinged with an undertone of awkwardness. 'Christine isn't home right now, but she'll be back soon. Would you like to come in and wait?'

Hailey hesitated, a maelstrom of thoughts and emotions racing through her mind. There was something different about him today, an openness that hadn't been there before.

'No—' she began to decline, but he persisted, a plea in his eyes.

'Please, just five minutes. It's important.'

After a brief internal struggle, Hailey relented. 'Okay, just five minutes,' she conceded, crossing the threshold into the house.

He gestured towards the living room. 'Make yourself comfortable. Can I get you something to drink?'

'No, thank you. I'm fine,' she replied, her voice betraying the nervousness that churned in her stomach as they settled into the living room.

Hailey glanced around the room, a sense of

displacement settling upon her. This was not a scenario she had ever anticipated: finding herself alone with Christine's husband again.

He shifted in his seat, his discomfort obvious. 'I want to apologize, Hailey. I realise I made you uncomfortable the last time you were here. That wasn't my intention.'

Hailey nodded, appreciating his candidness. 'I'm just relieved to know I wasn't imagining things.'

He sighed, his gaze momentarily dropping to his hands. 'No, you weren't. There's something I need to confess. It's been weighing on my mind.'

'What is it?'

Summoning a deep breath, he spoke, his voice trembling. 'I can't continue living without you knowing. Hailey, I … I love you.'

The words caught Hailey off guard. She instinctively stood, putting distance between them. 'What?'

Undeterred, he closed the physical gap, his eyes brimming with unshed tears. 'Every day, every moment that's passed, you've been on my mind … Hailey, you're my daughter.'

The world seemed to spin as Hailey processed his confession, struggling to make sense of it.

'What are you talking about?' she managed to utter, her voice shaky and uncertain.

He reached out, his hand trembling slightly as he gently rested it on her shoulder. 'I know this is overwhelming. I'm not asking for anything. I simply couldn't bear to keep this secret anymore. Christine felt it wasn't right to tell you after all this time—'

'H-how does Christine know?' Hailey's voice was barely more than a whisper, disbelief lacing her words.

'Because ... she's your mother.'

The revelation hit her like a tidal wave, emotions crashing over her in rapid succession – shock, confusion, disbelief, and an overwhelming sense of vulnerability. Hailey's eyes welled with tears, her heart torn between wanting to understand and the need to escape the weight of the moment.

She backed away, her body trembling as she reached for the door. 'I ... I can't. This is too much.'

Tears streamed down her cheeks as she turned and fled, the door closing behind her with a hushed finality. Hailey stood on the doorstep, the world a blur through the cascade of emotions that engulfed her.

What am I going to do now?

Chapter Sixty-Five

Sasha's heart raced as the doorbell echoed through the house. Glancing at Lindsay as she got up to answer the door, she tried to hide the nervous tremor in her hands. The social workers had arrived, and the reality of the situation hit Sasha hard. There was no turning back now. She had taken a stand, and now she had to face the consequences.

Sasha walked up behind her mother just as she opened the door. She saw her expression shifting from surprise to a composed façade. Two women stood on the doorstep, folders in hand.

'Good morning. We're from social services,' the older woman introduced herself, her voice calm and measured. 'We're here for a routine visit to check on Chloe Miller.'

Sasha's stomach dropped. This was it – the moment of truth. She reminded herself why she had taken this step. Chloe's well-being was more important than Lindsay's manipulation, and she had to believe that no matter the outcome.

As the social workers explained the purpose of their visit, their words felt distant, drowned out by the pounding of her heart. This was the right thing to do, wasn't it? Doubt gnawed at her, but she couldn't let it sway her resolve. Chloe deserved a better life, one free from her mother's control.

The social workers stepped into the living room, and Sasha's eyes darted between them and Lindsay. She knew the battle was just beginning, that Lindsay wouldn't give up her control without a fight.

Throughout the visit, she watched Lindsay's interactions closely, noting her attempts to maintain her façade. The social workers' questions, their observations, and their interactions with Chloe all felt like a spotlight on their lives.

When the social workers finally concluded their visit and left, the tension in the room was palpable.

Turning to Sasha, her mother's face was crimson. 'Why the fuck did you do this, Sasha? How fucking dare you do—'

'This is what you wanted, isn't it? I thought I'd just speed up the process for you. Chloe deserves better moth—'

Lindsay's anger flared. 'Chloe is my daughter, I—'

'No, that's where you're wrong. You may have given birth to her, but you are no mother!'

'What!? You're going to pay for this, I'll—'

Ignoring her mother's threats, Sasha turned and left the room. She had the ball in her court now; her mother's threats no longer had a grip on her life. Finally, she was free.

Chapter Sixty-Six

Hailey ignored her phone vibrating on the floor beside her bed. The caller's identity was no mystery – Christine. Hailey figured she must have returned home by now and Robert had likely spilled the truth. The truth that Christine had conveniently withheld for the entire year Hailey had known her. She took in a deep breath, the faint scent of weed wafting in through the open window.

It was difficult for Hailey to consider Christine as her mother. Not just because she had been given away as a child, but because Christine had woven a web of lies.

Her phone rang again, and she clenched her teeth in frustration. Maybe it was a good idea to turn it off. She wasn't exactly anticipating any important calls.

Why keep this from me? What could she have possibly gained from hiding the truth?

Each question only served to fuel her frustration and pain.

She had started to consider Christine like a second mother, someone she could confide in, laugh with, and trust implicitly. And now, the foundation of that trust had cracked, leaving Hailey feeling adrift.

Hailey's gaze shifted to the framed photo on her bedside table. It was a picture of her and Christine smiling during a hike at the residential camp they had attended. How many times had she looked at that photo, never suspecting the hidden truth lurking beneath the surface? It was so obvious now – she was the spitting image of her mother.

A sigh escaped Hailey's lips as she leaned back against the pillows.

I deserve to know. A spark of determination ignited within her. *I deserve to know the real reason behind all this.*

With newfound purpose, Hailey pushed herself off the bed.

Maybe it's time to confront her, not over the phone. In person.

Outside Christine's door, Hailey steeled herself, her hand poised to knock. She drew in a deep breath, urging herself to summon the strength to confront the truth that lay beyond the door.

The door creaked open, revealing Christine's warm smile, a stark contrast to the tempestuous thoughts swirling within Hailey's mind.

'Hailey … I … I've been trying to call you,' Christine began.

'Well, here I am. In person,' Hailey responded curtly. 'Come on then. I'm waiting to hear what you've got to say for yourself.'

Christine's expression turned earnest. 'I'm sorry—'

'Save it!' Hailey cut her off sharply. Apologies weren't what she needed right now; she needed answers, starting with why Christine had given her up.

It was as though Christine had sensed Hailey's thoughts, her voice taking on a tone of understanding.

'I owe it to you to tell you what happened from the beginning. Can we talk inside?'

Hailey's thoughts briefly flickered to Robert. She nodded in response to Christine's question. 'Is … he here?'

Christine nodded back. 'Robert's here.'

With a sense of determination, Hailey brushed past Christine and walked into the living room. Robert sat there, his hands resting on his head, as if he were bracing himself for the storm that was about to unfold.

'Hailey,' he began, his voice tinged with sorrow.

Hailey waved off his attempt to stand. 'Please don't get up.'

Christine followed her in, taking a seat next to Robert. Hailey's gaze shifted between them, her emotions a tangled mess.

'Okay,' Robert said. 'Before Christine begins, you have to believe us, Hailey. We love you more than anything in the world.'

Hailey's voice turned cold, her hurt evident. 'But not enough to keep me.'

'It wasn't like that. We didn't have a choice,' Christine interjected. 'I was only fourteen when you were born. I was still a kid myself. My parents gave me an ultimatum – have an abortion or give you up for adoption.

'We wanted to give you a chance at life. But it never got that far. I gave birth at home; it was so unexpected … I lost a lot of blood, by the time I came round … you were gone. My mum said you'd died.' The words stumbled over one another, as if they'd finally been released from their bondage.

Hailey's anger wavered slightly, replaced by confusion and sadness. 'Why, why would she tell you that?'

Christine's eyes glistened with unshed tears. 'To make it easier for me, I suppose. It was only on her deathbed that she finally told me the truth. That she'd given you away to her cousin.'

'Maggie was her cousin?'

'Yes. We tried to find her, to find you, but—'

'We didn't know …' Robert's voice cracked, his face etched with pain. 'We didn't know her cousin had passed away, and by then it was too late. It took us this long to finally find you.'

Hailey's anger began to ebb. She saw the pain etched on her parents' faces, the regret they carried for a decision made for them.

'Why didn't you just tell me the truth? Why keep it a secret?'

Tears streamed down Christine's cheeks. 'I was scared, Hailey. Scared that knowing the truth would change how you saw me, how you felt about me. I thought I could protect you from that pain.'

Hailey's shoulders sagged as the storm of her emotions began to subside. She sank into a nearby chair, her eyes tired but her heart still in turmoil. 'You should have trusted me enough to tell me. I deserved to know the truth about my own life.'

She looked between Christine and Robert, her heart aching with conflicting feelings.

'I thought you were my friend.'

Christine reached out, her hand hovering in the air before she hesitantly touched Hailey's arm. 'I should've told you, Hailey. I should've found the courage to tell you what had happened.'

The room fell into a heavy silence.

'We're so sorry,' Robert's voice broke the silence.

Christine nodded, her voice a whisper. 'We understand if you're angry with us, if you need time to process all of this.'

Hailey felt a wave of emotions crashing over her – anger, hurt, but also a flicker of understanding. The revelation didn't erase the years of absence, but it painted a different shade of complexity onto her history. As she looked at the two people before her, her heart wavered between resentment and the remnants of a bond she hadn't realised she still held. Hailey met Christine's gaze, the words on the tip of her tongue. But as she looked into Christine's eyes, something held her back. The connection they had shared over the last year, the memories they had created together – it wasn't something Hailey was ready to let go of.

Chapter Sixty-Seven

'Listen,' Jo began. 'I want to prepare you for what you're about to hear. It's not going to be easy.'

'I don't care,' Sasha said. 'I want to hear it. I'm sure she's not going to say anything that hasn't been said before.'

With careful precision, Jo inserted the drive into her laptop and initiated a sequence of actions. Within moments, Lindsay's voice emanated from the speakers, filling the room with a heavy atmosphere. Sasha sat with her head slightly bowed. She felt a pang of empathy for Hailey, imagining the immense strength it took for her to endure listening to her mother telling her that she basically used her.

The recording played out, and its conclusion left an echoing silence. The weight of the revelations settled in, rendering everyone speechless for a brief, contemplative pause.

Breaking the silence, Sasha's voice was full of accusation. 'Dad, how much of this did you already know?'

Josh let out a weary sigh, his gaze fixed on the floor as if searching for the right words. 'More than I'd like to admit, Sasha. I was aware of some of your mother's lies, her plans. I thought I could somehow mitigate the fallout, shield you and Chloe from the worst of it.'

'But why, Dad? Why did you let it continue?'

Josh's eyes conveyed a deep well of remorse. 'I've always carried guilt within me. Guilt for letting Miles be put up for adoption all those years ago. I believed that by supporting Lindsay, I could make amends, create a better life for you and Chloe.'

'That's hardly an excuse,' Sasha retorted, her emotions raw. 'It didn't make life better for us. My existence was a nightmare until I met Hailey.'

Josh's voice wavered, laden with pain. 'I'm well aware of my shortcomings. I'm nothing but a weak and inadequate man.'

Jo interjected with sigh of exasperation. 'Oh, come on, Josh. Pity parties aren't going to change anything. If anyone should be tired of them, it's you. It's time to step up, face the mess you played a part in creating.'

Josh looked up at Jo, defeat in his eyes. 'How?'

Miles, previously quiet, chose that moment to interject, his voice brimming with confidence.

'I know how,' he declared, capturing everyone's attention. 'We confront her.'

Sasha leaned back in her chair, her arms crossed. 'Confronting her is one thing, but what do you suggest we do beyond that? Just shaming her might not make much of a difference at this point. She's already lost everything. She barely leaves the house anymore except to go to church.'

Miles considered Sasha's words for a moment before responding. 'You're right. Shaming her might not be the solution. But there's more to this than just making her feel bad. It's about acknowledging the truth and letting other people who may still be under her influence know.'

Jo chimed in, her voice thoughtful. 'Holding onto these secrets has taken a toll on all of us. Bringing everything out into the open might finally offer some closure and a chance to move forward.'

Sasha's eyes shifted from one face to another around the table. There was a complexity to the situation that she was beginning to see more clearly. 'So, we're not just doing this for her, but for us.'

Jo smiled softly. 'Exactly.'

Sasha leaned forward. 'All right, then. Let's do it. But where?'

'I know just the place,' Josh said.

Chapter Sixty-Eight

Sasha sat in the quiet sanctuary of the church, the wooden pew beneath her hard against her legs. Beside her, Lindsay and Josh sat, tension and uncertainty emanating from them.

As the service began, Sasha's mind was far from the hymns being sung. She couldn't shake the weight of the recent revelations: her mother's deceit, her father's hidden guilt, the existence of a long-lost brother. It was as if her entire world had been turned upside down, and now she found herself in this sacred space, grappling with her emotions and seeking a way forward.

The service continued, prayers and sermons filling the air. Then, without warning, Josh rose from his seat, his gaze fixed on the pulpit at the front of the church. Sasha's heart raced as he walked purposefully towards the podium, a determined expression on his face.

He paused for a moment, his eyes scanning the faces of those in attendance. Then, with a steady hand, he produced his phone and connected it to the church's sound system. The room fell into an expectant hush as he pressed play.

The voice that filled the church was unmistakable: Lindsay's voice, the recording Hailey had made.

Gasps rippled through the congregation as her words echoed off the walls, the truth of her lies laid bare for all to hear. Sasha watched as her mother's face turned ashen, shock and disbelief washing over her features.

Without a word, Lindsay attempted to rise from her seat, as if the weight of her own words had become too much to bear. But Sasha acted on instinct, her hand reaching out and gripping her mother's arm gently but firmly. Lindsay turned to Sasha, their eyes locking in a silent struggle.

Sasha's grip loosened slightly, but her voice was unwavering. 'No, Mum. You can't run from this anymore. You have to face it, all of it.'

Lindsay's lips trembled, her eyes glistening as she sat back down.

'I want redemption …' Josh said when the recording came to a stop. His eyes locked on Lindsay. 'For us both. And what better place to seek it than the house of God?'

Tears welled up in Sasha's eyes as she watched her father, a man who had been complicit in the deception, now taking a stand for truth and redemption.

All eyes were on Lindsay, whose façade of strength had crumbled in the face of her own words. She looked smaller, more vulnerable than Sasha had ever seen her.

Sasha glanced around at the faces of those in the pews, a mixture of shock, empathy, and curiosity etched on their features. The truth had been exposed and there was no turning back.

As Josh stepped away from the pulpit, returning to his seat beside Sasha, she felt a renewed sense of connection with him. The rift that had formed between them seemed to be closing, replaced by a shared desire to confront the past and rebuild their relationship.

In that moment, as the church held its collective breath, Sasha realised that even amidst the chaos and pain, there was a chance for healing. And as Lindsay's gaze met hers, anger, regret, and something resembling vulnerability shone in her eyes, Sasha knew that their journey towards redemption had only just begun.

Chapter Sixty-Nine

As the days turned into months, Hailey's manuscript underwent revisions and edits. She poured her heart and soul into every word, ensuring that her story would resonate with others who had faced their own challenges. The book became a symbol of her resilience, a testament to her ability to rise above the darkness that had threatened to engulf her.

And when the day of the book's release arrived, Hailey stood before a crowd of eager readers, her heart pounding with excitement and nervousness. As she spoke about her journey, about the process of reclaiming her narrative, she felt a sense of catharsis, a release of the emotions that had held her captive for so long.

As Hailey signed copies of her book, she looked up and was taken aback at the sight of Sasha approaching tentatively, a silent apology in her eyes.

'I'm sorry,' Sasha whispered, her voice barely audible over the din of the crowd.

Hailey's gaze softened, and for a moment, the weight of their shared history hung between them. 'It'll take time.'

And as they stood there, amidst the buzz of the book launch, Hailey realised that her story was no longer defined by Lindsay's deceit or Sasha's betrayal. It was a story of resilience, of finding strength in the face of adversity, and of rebuilding relationships on the foundation of authenticity.

As the event wound down, Hailey found herself stealing glances at Sasha from across the room. She couldn't deny the ache that still lingered, the memories of their time together that danced at the edges of her mind. The love she had felt hadn't simply disappeared; it had transformed into a bittersweet yearning.

Eventually, the crowd began to disperse, and Hailey found herself alone, surrounded by the remnants of her successful book launch. That's when she felt a presence beside her, and turning, she met Sasha's gaze once more.

'Hailey,' Sasha began, her voice hesitant yet filled with an underlying sincerity. 'I know I hurt you, and I can't erase the past, but I want you to know that I've changed. I've learned from my mistakes, and I'm ready to be the person you deserve.'

Hailey studied Sasha's eyes, seeing the vulnerability that lay beneath the surface. She took a deep breath, her heart torn between caution and the longing she still felt. 'Sasha, I … I miss you.'

The admission lingered in the air, a fragile bridge between their broken past and the uncertain future. And then, as if guided by an unspoken understanding, they both began to laugh, the tension dissipating.

'What's so funny?' Hailey asked, a smile playing on her lips.

Sasha's eyes sparkled with affection. 'We've been through so much – secrets, pain, and now a book launch. Our story sounds like a soap opera.'

Hailey giggled, a warmth spreading through her chest. 'Well, it would make an awesome book.'

Sasha stepped closer, her hand reaching out to brush against Hailey's.

'Hailey, I know we can't rewrite our history, but maybe we can start a new chapter.'

And then, with a tenderness that spoke volumes, Hailey leaned in, their lips meeting in a kiss that held all the longing, all the apologies, and all the possibilities they had kept hidden for so long.

As Hailey looked into Sasha's eyes, she saw a reflection of her own hopes and fears. The pain of the past was still there, but it was overshadowed by the potential for something beautiful.

'Okay,' Hailey said softly, pulling Sasha close. 'A new chapter.'

Chapter Seventy

The dining table was bathed in the soft glow of flickering candles, its surface graced by the remnants of their hearty roast dinner. The aroma of cooked meats and roasted vegetables still lingered in the air, a reminder of the delicious meal they had shared earlier.

'To new beginnings,' Hailey said, raising her wine glass in the air.

Sasha clinked her glass against Hailey's. 'And to finally having our own home.'

'I'm just excited about having a big kitchen. Maybe I won't burn my experiments next time.'

'I'm counting on it.' Sasha gave her a playful nudge.

Hailey grinned and mock saluted. 'No more burnt offerings, I promise.'

Miles, sat opposite, leaned back in his chair, his gaze drifting upwards. 'Who would've thought we'd all end up here together.'

'Life works in mysterious ways,' Christine said.

There was a moment of silence as they reflected on their journey and the bonds that had formed. The roller-coaster from hell they'd all been on had finally given way to calmer waters. And for the first time, in what seemed her whole life, Sasha could actually relax without having to keep looking over her shoulder, not knowing what to expect next.

Robert turned to Hailey, a grin on his face. 'So, Hailey, how's that story you've been talking about coming along?'

Hailey's eyes lit up. 'It's coming together really well.'

'What's it about?' Miles said.

'Unexpected connections, secrets that bind us, and the power of forgiveness.'

Jo leaned in. 'Sounds interesting. Are there characters based on us?'

Hailey winked, a mischievous grin playing on her lips. 'Definitely. They say real life is stranger than fiction.'

As dessert was served, Jo turned to Josh. 'Speaking of real life, any news from Lindsay?'

Josh shook his head, a sense of finality in his tone. 'Nope and I'm happy not to ever hear from her again.' Josh looked at Chloe fast asleep in her pram next to him. 'I always knew she had it in her to up and leave when the going got tough, but I never thought she'd leave Chloe behind.'

'That didn't surprise me at all,' Sasha said sadly. 'But I think it's for the best.'

Her mother hadn't even said goodbye. One minute she was there, and the next, every one of her belongings had been removed from the house while Sasha was at university and Josh was at work. All that remained was a signed form on the kitchen table giving Josh full custody of Chloe. No explanation, no apology. Nothing. Sasha liked to think that somewhere in that cold heart of her mother's, she did love them in her own way, but she doubted it. She had to keep telling herself that some people are just unable to love, and that it was okay because there were plenty of people who could and did. And those people that mattered were sitting around the table with her.

'I wouldn't put it past Lindsay to be holed up somewhere writing her next book under a new name,' Jo said.

Miles raised his glass, a smirk on his face. 'Well, at least we have one less source of drama now. And I've finally got my real family right here.'

Jo placed her hand on Miles's shoulder, her smile tender. 'We've always been your family, Miles.'

Later, in the quiet of the night, Hailey slipped into bed next to Sasha with a grin.

'I've got a thought,' Hailey began.

Sasha raised an eyebrow, a playful glint in her eye. 'Oh boy, what's brewing?'

'What if I sneak some of our conversations from tonight into my story?'

Sasha widened her eyes in mock shock. 'Oh no, you'd spill the beans on the not-so-cute stories my dad told you about me?'

Hailey burst into laughter, the sound filling the room. 'I can't resist, it's too good!'

Wrapped in each other's arms, as the laughter faded, Sasha couldn't help but feel that their story – with its ups and downs – was worth telling, not just through words on paper, but through the moments they continued to create together.

Chapter Seventy-One

The bookstore buzzed with the gentle hum of anticipation as Lindsay stood poised before the podium. This was her moment. A fresh start on her own terms this time, no baggage to weigh her down. A whole new makeover with a change of name and new appearance – she had metamorphosed into a different person, on the outside anyway. She was now ready to share her words with an audience untouched by her past.

As Lindsay began reading from her latest self-published book, her gaze swept the crowd, keen and observant. In the front row, a woman caught her attention – attentive, engrossed, hanging onto each word. After the reading, Lindsay greeted attendees with nods and smiles as they formed a line for book signings.

Last in line was the woman Lindsay had noticed earlier. As she approached, her eyes brightened as she presented her book for Lindsay's signature.

'Your writing is amazing. The way you interweave complex lives and emotions ... it's mind-blowing.'

Lindsay responded with a modest smile. 'Thank you. Real-life stories fascinate me. So, what do you do?'

'I'm the CEO of a finance company.'

Lindsay took in the woman's expensive clothes and the large diamond ring on her finger. 'That's impressive.'

A bittersweet smile graced the woman's lips. 'It

wasn't easy to achieve. I was homeless for many years, living in my car, fighting to survive. But with the grace of God, I persevered, and managed to get a university degree.'

Lindsay's interest deepened. 'Wow, that sounds like an incredible journey.'

The woman nodded, her eyes holding Lindsay's. 'Believe me, it did. But I worked around studying, with twelve-hour shifts cleaning offices at night.'

Leaning in, Lindsay's tone brimmed with empathy, she asked, 'Would you be open to sharing more of your story? It's very inspiring, and I'd like to learn more.'

Pausing, the woman's expression turned contemplative. 'I'd love to.'

Though Lindsay's smile remained a fixture on her face, her mind raced ahead, sketching plans for her next book. 'That's great. Let's swap numbers and catch up soon.'

With the signing session coming to an end, Lindsay left the bookstore. As she ventured into the night, the echo of her footsteps dissolved into the shadows.

Nothing was going to halt her relentless pursuit of the person she believed she was destined to be. With the old life left behind and a new one beckoning, Lindsay was on a one-way journey to greener pastures, heedless of the wreckage she had left in her wake.

Follow Jade

Newsletter: www.jade-winters.com

Twitter: @jadewinters16

Instagram: @jadewinters

Facebook: www.facebook.com/jadewintersauthor/

Printed in Great Britain
by Amazon